"I need a man,"

Olivia told the handsome stranger.

"Ah, the liberated approach." He nodded encouragingly. "I like that type. They usually split the check."

"No—I mean only for a few minutes...."

"A busy career woman on the go, eh?"

"I need a man to pretend to be my husband. It's a long story. Oh, and it's too late now."

Marsha swept into the room. "Here you are, Olivia. And this must be the man I've heard so much about."

Olivia wished with all her heart and soul that the floor would open up and swallow her. Just as she was contemplating a mad dash out the door, the man at her side spoke.

"And Olivia has told me all about you, too," he said in his husky baritone.

Dear Reader,

Welcome to Silhouette! Our goal is to give you hours of unbeatable reading pleasure, and we hope you'll enjoy each month's six new Silhouette Desires. These sensual, provocative love stories are both believable and compelling—sometimes they're poignant, sometimes humorous, but always enjoyable.

Indulge yourself. Experience all the passion and excitement of falling in love along with our heroine as she meets the irresistible man of her dreams and together they overcome all obstacles in the path to a happy ending.

If this is your first Desire, I hope it'll be the first of many. If you're already a Silhouette Desire reader, thanks for your support! Look for some of your favorite authors in the coming months: Stephanie James, Diana Palmer, Dixie Browning, Ann Major and Doreen Owens Malek, to name just a few.

Happy reading!

Isabel Swift
Senior Editor

SDRL-7/85

ANNE CAVALIERE
Perfect Timing

Silhouette Desire

Published by Silhouette Books New York

America's Publisher of Contemporary Romance

SILHOUETTE BOOKS
300 East 42nd St., New York, N.Y. 10017

Copyright © 1987 by Anne Canadeo

ISBN: 0-373-05328-2

First Silhouette Books printing January 1987

America's Publisher of Contemporary Romance

Printed in the U.S.A.

ANNE CAVALIERE

worked as a reporter in Denver and Minneapolis before turning to writing fiction as a full-time career. She's also held various positions in the field of advertising in New York. Her interests include sailing, antiques and eavesdropping. She presently lives in Sea Cliff, a small village on the Long Island Sound.

One

The big, dark-haired man at the end of the bar was her last hope. Olivia Grant had been wandering around the hotel, dressed to kill, for more than two hours and she hadn't come across one man who even vaguely suited her needs.

It wasn't that she had failed to attract male attention. Far from it. She had passed on no less than eight propositions since half-past six, which had to be some personal record breaker. Four of her would-be suitors had used approaches that fell into the pleasant and civilized category. Three had been what she would diplomatically term straightforward and direct. The last, coming from a man old enough to be her grandfather, had been downright raunchy. Unfortunately, civilized or not, not one of these men had been the type she was looking for. Olivia half expected the house detective to introduce himself at any moment. At this point, even that horrendous fate would have been some relief.

With only fifteen minutes to go, Olivia considered herself lucky to finally find a man who fit the description almost exactly. He was alone, sipping a beer, and watching a football game on the wide-screen TV over the bar. There was an empty seat next to him and she headed straight for it.

As she approached him she could see that her suspect prey looked like a typical businessman on an out-of-town trip. He wore a slightly rumpled, yet fine quality, navy-blue suit. His red silk tie was loosened at the collar. He looked a bit bored, like a man with an empty evening stretching before him who preferred to watch the football game in a crowded bar, rather than in a drab, empty hotel room. Maybe he would consider her proposition an amusing way to pass the time, the makings of a laughable anecdote to tell the folks back home.

At the age of thirty-two, Olivia had certainly had her share of chance meetings with the opposite sex. Still, picking up men in hotel bars was not exactly her style. For heaven's sake, you're an actress, aren't you? she prodded herself. Well, go out there and act. After taking a deep breath and straightening the plunging neckline of her dress, Olivia gamely forged ahead.

"Uh—excuse me." Olivia pulled out the stool next to her target and smiled engagingly. "This seat isn't taken, is it?"

He glanced at her casually and shifted his stool over to make room. "It's all yours."

Olivia sat down and gave him another, even more dazzling, smile. He smiled back this time—a bit too briefly, she thought with dismay—then looked up again at the TV. Somehow he looked more intimidating close up than he had from across the room. He sat moodily hunched over his beer, his broad shoulders straining the fabric of his jacket.

Olivia reconsidered for an instant. She glanced around. There were no other suitable candidates in sight and it was only fifteen minutes until her 9:00 p.m. deadline. She could either show up in the lobby with a man in tow, or find the rear exit to this hotel and catch the first flight back to New York. After all these years, it was still a question of pride between herself and Marsha Mott Carmichael. She had gone this far with this ridiculous situation; Olivia decided that she couldn't back down now.

"What will it be ma'am?" The bartender wiped the area in front of her and set down a red cocktail napkin. "Gin gimlet, please," she ordered automatically. "Uh...on second thought, forget that. That beer you're having really looks great," she said to the man next to her, "I think I'll have one, too."

Again, he turned toward her, this time looking her up and down with a slow, assessing glance. When his eyes met hers, Olivia could tell she had passed inspection. At least this particular fish has some interest in the bait, she comforted herself.

The bartender then rattled off the names of at least nine different brands of beer, some foreign, some domestic, none of which sounded the least bit appetizing to Olivia. She actually hated the taste of beer and hadn't touched the stuff since high school.

"What kind are you having?" she asked her neighbor.

"The imported light. On tap."

"Oh, that sounds good. I'll have one, too," she told the bartender.

She turned back to her prey to see that he was watching her with a quizzical expression in his eyes. Maybe he isn't used to having women try to pick him up, she thought. Yet, she could not quite accept that as a plausible explanation. He wasn't good looking, not in the typical way at least, but he certainly did have a quality that made him stand out from all the other men around her. A quality she was sure many women found appealing.

With his large frame and brooding expression, he looked as if he could be very fierce when crossed, but at the same time very protective and comforting to those he considered his own. His face was broad, with high cheekbones and an angular jaw, his chin marked by a cleft that seemed even more prominent because of his slight, five o'clock shadow. His nose was a trifle bent, Olivia noticed, as if it had been broken long ago and improperly set. He had straight white teeth and quite an attractive smile... when he cared to use it. So far, that had been rarely. Not a good sign at all, Olivia thought.

The beer appeared before her in a long, cool-looking glass. Olivia could sense her neighbor observing her every motion. With an enthusiasm she certainly did not feel, she lifted the glass and turned toward him. "Cheers," she said, taking a hearty gulp.

It tasted just as she remembered from those basement parties of her tender, teenage years. Awful, like soapy water with just a dash of nail polish remover tossed in for color. Time had certainly not improved her taste for distilled malt and hops. Olivia was seized by an overwhelming urge to gag but valiantly fought it off. Glancing at her newfound friend she had the uneasy feeling that he realized her predicament and was fighting the urge to laugh.

She dabbed delicately at her mouth with the cocktail napkin, trying to remove the foam mustache while still salvaging some remnant of lip gloss. He looked as if he was waiting for her to say something.

"Great beer," she offered finally. "Nice and... light."

"Yes, it is, uh... light," he agreed. He just kept looking at her. This was not going to be easy, she thought. Not easy at all. Of all the men in this hotel, she had to pick the strong, silent type. She glanced at her watch. Less than ten minutes to go. Olivia urged herself to pick up the pace.

"How's the game tonight?" She glanced up at the TV screen, which now pictured a massive pile of huge male bodies, legs and arms jutting out at various painful-looking angles. The players were beginning to untangle themselves and line up in formation on the startlingly green playing field. Olivia knew next to nothing about football and hadn't the slightest urge to learn more. The sport was violent and moronic. The fact that these men received such outlandishly high salaries for running up and down a field, trying to maim each other, was morally reprehensible to her.

"Fantastic game," her dark-haired companion replied. The genuine fervor of a true fan was unmistakable in his tone. Olivia silently winced. "The Cowboys just lost ten yards on a penalty, but they've had two sacks and three intercepts in the last quarter," he reported.

As far as Olivia was concerned, he might have been speaking a foreign language. If his gaze had not been fixed on the screen, he would surely have noticed the dazed expression on her face. The ball was in flight and some lumbering giant, number twenty-three, caught it and began to run like the devil down field. Two other gargantuan types, from the opposing team, Olivia assumed, caught up with him, jumped all over the poor man and dragged him down to the ground. Number twenty-three valiantly clutched the ball to his chest throughout the entire onslaught. A whistle blew and Olivia felt as if a knot had formed in her stomach simply from watching.

"That guy has got the greatest hands in the league," her companion enthused.

"He's got fantastic hands all right," Olivia agreed, feeling as if she had just made some intimate confession about her personal life. She smiled at him again and brought her beer glass to her lips, pretending to take a small sip.

"Watch much football?" His eyes were not brown, as she had first thought, but hazel, with small flecks of gold.

"Sure—hardly miss a game," she said casually.

"Is that so?" He gave her one of his rare smiles then, dimples appearing in each of his lean cheeks. He would do perfectly, Olivia thought. Better than she had a right to expect, in fact.

"Which club do you follow?" he asked, interrupting her thoughts.

"Which club?" She belonged to the Sierra Club. And the League of Women Voters...but hadn't they been talking about football?

Her friend smiled to himself and picked through a bowl of mixed nuts on the bar between them. He came up with a large cashew and popped it into his mouth. "Do you have a favorite team, I mean."

"Oh...well I'm from New York so I guess I do feel partial to—"for the life of her Olivia could not recall the name of one New York football team"—to the hometown club," she finished lamely.

"How civic-minded of you." He sounded vaguely amused and not very convinced.

Before Olivia had the chance to embarrass herself further, a roar erupted from the TV and they both looked up to check the action on the screen. Number twenty-three, looking a bit worse for wear, Olivia thought, was running down field with the ball again, this time cleverly eluding those trying to tackle him. Nimbly twisting and turning out of their grasp, he reached the end of the field with the ball safely tucked under one arm. Even Olivia knew he had scored. The whole bar was in an uproar, echoing the televised cheers of the fans in the stadium.

"My God! Did you see that man run?" Her companion was up off his seat and for an instant gripped her arm in his excitement. "That must have been eighty yards at least. I can't believe it."

He had only touched her lightly, without thinking, but in that brief touch she could sense his considerable strength. "That was really something," Olivia agreed, caught up in his elation. The score flashed on the screen and Olivia could see that the two teams were now tied. "Gosh, one more homer like that and they'll have the lead," she offered sagely.

He turned and looked at her. "Touchdown, you mean?"

"Oh, right." She laughed. "Of course, how silly of me." She took a handful of nuts and munched nervously, not daring to look up at him.

"You don't know anything about football, do you?" he asked quietly.

Olivia felt a peanut stick in her throat and she gulped it down. "I couldn't tell a tight end from a split end, if you really want to know the truth."

She finally looked up at him. He still wasn't smiling but he wasn't exactly *not* smiling, either.

"You're not crazy about beer, either, are you?" He gestured toward the glass, which had remained relatively untouched.

Olivia stared back at him thoughtfully for a moment. "I consider it absolute swill," she confessed.

He laughed. "Now we're getting somewhere."

"We are?"

"I knew something was up the minute I spotted you in the doorway, lining up your ducks."

"My ducks?"

"Look, you're not exactly dressed for a night of beer and peanuts."

"How observant of you." She was in fact wearing an obscenely expensive masterfully understated black silk dinner dress, black lace stockings and diamond stud earrings. "But I think you may be jumping to the wrong conclusions here, Sherlock."

"Hey, it's a great-looking dress." He looked her up and down again with an appreciative male gleam in his eye. Then he tossed a few peanuts into his mouth. "Don't get me wrong."

"Thanks," she said curtly. She picked up her black snakeskin clutch, which had also cost a small fortune, and eased off the stool. What had ever made her think that this harebrained scheme would work out? It certainly wasn't going to work with this man, that was for sure. When it came to choosing men—choosing men for *anything*—why were her instincts invariably awful?

"Leaving so soon? Things are just getting interesting around here. Plenty of ball game left...as they say." Holding her gaze, he cocked his head toward the screen.

"Unfortunately, for some of us the clock has just about run out," Olivia mumbled. She took some bills from her purse and placed them on the bar next to her glass.

"Sure I couldn't get you something else to drink? A gin gimlet, wasn't it?"

He was being charming now and the sudden change of manner caught her by surprise. Even though he had mistaken her intentions—probably thought she made a profession out of this kind of thing—he definitely had what she called potential.

"Sorry. I have to meet some old friends for a drink and I'm already late." A drink and the most embarrassing moment of my life, she amended silently.

"Old friends, eh?" he said with eyebrows raised. He shrugged. "Maybe next time then. My name is Jonas, by the way."

"Olivia," she offered. He really did have the nicest smile. But if she remained here even a few moments more, she was sure that Marsha would track her down. The thing to do was get out of sight, the sooner the better, until she decided whether she wanted to face down Marsha and Brad or bolt herself in her room. Neither alternative seemed particularly attractive at the moment.

When she looked back at Jonas, he was staring at her curiously. "Well, so long, Olivia...have a nice evening."

"Thanks. Have a nice life." Olivia turned on her very high, black heels and made her way toward the exit.

There, coming through the light-filled doorway she spotted the sole source of her predicament, Marsha Mott Carmichael—ex-college roommate, ex-best friend, wife of entrepreneur extraordinaire and the woman who had stolen away Olivia's fiancé during their senior year of college.

They had not laid eyes on each other for more than ten years, and in all truth, Olivia had put the past neatly behind her. But that very afternoon, when Marsha loomed up before her in the hotel lobby, bragging about Brad's career, their children and their houses, the old feelings of trying to compete with Marsha and always ending up second best came rushing back.

Marsha and Olivia had verbally sparred like two fencers, two old antagonists who knew each other's tricks and weaknesses only too well. Olivia had kept up her end of the match admirably, not exactly bragging, but making the most of the successes she had seen so far in her acting career. Her life in Manhattan sounded far more glamorous than it actually was. Olivia had, in fact, come to Southern California looking for work. The character she played in a daytime soap was about to be killed off by unnatural causes—and so was Olivia's contract.

Marsha heard none of this; according to Olivia, her life was the glitzy, sequin-spangled dream of every bored Midwestern housewife. The duel was evenly matched for a while, each parry met with a thrust and an equally deadly smile. Until Marsha decided to ask the unaskable—a question cruelly calculated to deal Olivia the ultimate humiliating blow. Until that moment Olivia had forgotten just how tacky Marsha could be when backed into a corner. That is, until she smirked and said, "So, dear...did you *ever* get married?"

Olivia, who had kept good control of her emotions until that point, suddenly saw red. She looked right into the tinted-blue contact lenses of her expensively dressed adversary and did what any other self-respecting woman would have done in that position. She lied.

After Brad Carmichael there had been a number of men who had wanted to join their fortunes with Olivia's. But for one reason or another, she had never felt inclined to take that final, momentous step. Olivia had never once considered being single the least cause for embarrassment. To many of the married people she knew her freedom was considered an enviable position. But when Marsha posed the question, the issue took on another dimension entirely. After all, Marsha was the grand prizewinner in the "Marry Brad Carmichael Sweepstakes," while Olivia had only been first runner-up.

All things considered, that first lie had been easy. Creating Super Spouse on the spot had been great fun for Olivia. Producing him in the flesh, however, was another story entirely. If she had been home in Manhattan she might have called any one of a dozen friends to help her out. But she wasn't in New York. She was in a town where she knew virtually no one. Olivia had never meant to agree to meet Brad and Marsha for a drink and actually produce the fantasy husband but somehow Marsha had gotten to her. She always did have a way of talking circles around everyone else, of getting them so confused they didn't know what they were agreeing to.

In her own defense Olivia could only plead temporary insanity. After the dust had cleared, the logical thing to do would have been to call the Carmichaels and make up some plausible excuse. Or to check out of the hotel, leaving some appropriately apologetic note behind. Olivia had even composed several notes, which she crumpled and tossed in the wastebasket, one by one. The temptation to show up on the arm of some attractive, impressive man—if only for five minutes—had been far too great. Olivia realized now that she had deluded herself into thinking she could persuade someone to play along with her.

Marsha had definitely spotted her, and Olivia watched as her old classmate made her way through the maze of cocktail tables. Olivia felt like a small animal, mesmerized by the headlights of an oncoming truck. Acting on sheer instinct, she walked rapidly back to the bar and tapped Jonas on the shoulder.

He turned, surprise and even some pleasure flickering in his eyes. "Couldn't stay away, eh?"

"I have to ask you something," she said quickly.

"I thought that was it the first time you sat down." He grinned at her knowingly.

Olivia shook her head. "This is not what you think—"

"I think you're a little nuts—in a totally charming way, of course—if you really want to know the truth."

"Stop interrupting me, will you please?" she hissed. She took a deep breath. "I need a man," she began to explain.

"Ah, the liberated approach," he said nodding encouragingly. "I like that type. They usually split the check."

"No—I mean only for a few minutes . . ."

"A busy career woman on the go, eh?"

"I need a man to pretend to be my husband. It's a long story. I can't explain right now."

Jonas took in the wild expression in her brown eyes, the flush on her cheeks, the attractive disarray of her wavy, layer-cut red hair. She was one enticing woman, that was for sure. But he was damned if he could figure out what was going on here.

"I can just imagine," he said finally.

"I sincerely doubt it." Olivia glanced quickly over her shoulder. Marsha was just a few steps away. "Oh, damn," she cursed under her breath. "Too late."

"I thought I saw you two hiding back here." Marsha appeared beside them and smiled. She glanced from Olivia to Jonas and then back to Olivia again. "I thought the four of us were supposed to meet in the lobby at nine. I'm so glad I found you."

Olivia wished with all her heart that the floor would open up and swallow her whole. No such luck. Now it was too late to even skulk back up to her room and hide out. She was faced with the choice of making up a bigger and even more unbelievable lie to explain the regrettable absence of her "husband," or making a full confession. True, dashing madly for the door was another possibility. But she had the feeling Marsha would come after her and tackle her down, like one of those running backs she had just watched on TV.

"Marsha! Is it nine already?" Olivia looked down at her watch, stalling for time.

Jonas glanced from the tall, pencil-thin blonde to the attractive—albeit zany—redhead. His intuition told him that it wasn't the redhead's style to give up so easily. He had always harbored a special fondness for the underdog—not to mention for crazy redheads. Without considering the possible consequences, he slipped off the bar stool and draped his arm possessively across Olivia's bare shoulder.

"Sorry for the delay, Marsha," he said in his most charming manner. "Poor Olivia just couldn't drag me away from the football game. Isn't that right, honey?"

Incredulous, Olivia slowly turned to look at the man beside her. He answered her astounded gaze with an intimate little wink and a hug. He was not as tall as Olivia had first thought, but what he lacked in height, he more than made up for in sheer physical presence.

"You know you didn't even mention your husband's name when we met today, Olivia," Marsha scolded in a friendly manner. "I'm sure I would have remembered," she apologized sweetly to Jonas.

"Oh, I'm sorry...I didn't, did I? Marsha, this is...my husband, Jonas." She waited tensely for a lightning bolt to strike her dead, or perhaps for some less dramatic sign of divine displeasure.

Jonas smiled, displaying his dimples and straight white teeth to full advantage. Olivia watched as Marsha responded, coyly smiling back when Jonas took her hand. "I'm very pleased to meet you," he said smoothly.

"And I'm simply delighted to meet you. Olivia's told me so little about you, Jonas...."

Jonas gazed down at his wife with an amused smile hovering at the corners of his lips. "Olivia is like that. She loves to have her little secrets."

"Well, it will be fun for us to get acquainted, don't you think?" Marsha rattled on. "Why the three of us—Olivia, Brad and I—haven't been together like this in years. I suppose this is kind of a reunion for us. Wouldn't you say, Olivia?"

"I guess you could call it that," Olivia agreed with forced brightness.

"I was just saying to Brad," Marsha continued, "it reminds me a little of that movie...I can't think of the name now. You know, the one where the old college friends get together?"

"*Death Wish*?" Olivia offered quietly.

"Pardon?" Marsha had not heard her over the noise in the bar, but Jonas had.

"You mean *The Big Chill*," he cut in diplomatically. He glanced from one woman to the other. He still couldn't figure out what was going on here, but he was willing to bet that the story was a beauty.

"Yes, that's the one." Marsha beamed with relief. "Brad couldn't remember, either." She smiled gratefully at Jonas. "How clever of you, Jonas."

Some people never change, Olivia silently fumed. "Where is dear old Brad?" she asked abruptly.

"He's waiting for us in the restaurant lounge." Marsha lifted her wrist and glanced at a watch that Olivia knew cost about as much as the down payment on her apartment. "Oh, dear. Look at the time. You know how Brad hates to wait. Shall we go?"

Without waiting for their reply, Marsha began walking briskly toward the exit. As they passed through the crowded lobby, it was difficult to walk together. They soon became separated from Marsha when she took a sharp turn around a potted palm and disappeared from sight. Olivia gripped Jonas's wrist and held him back.

"Hold it a second. I nearly forgot something." Jonas watched as she slipped a small gold band out of her purse and onto the ring finger of her left hand. "Here's yours," she said, handing him the matching mate. He held the ring in the palm of his hand and stared down at it.

"You must have been some Girl Scout, Olivia," he commented dryly.

"It's really my favorite pair of earrings," she explained, ignoring his barb, "so don't lose it. Hopefully, I can bend them back into shape when this is all over. Well?" she said impatiently, noticing that he hadn't made a move to put it on.

"Do I have to? I mean, a lot of men don't wear wedding rings."

"I might have guessed you were *that* type. You probably have a real wife and twelve kids stashed away somewhere, don't you?"

"Don't be ridiculous. Of course I don't. Here," he said, trying to jam the band on his finger. "If it makes you happy, I'll wear it. The blasted thing doesn't even fit."

"Let me help you." Olivia removed the ring, stretched it wider and slipped it on Jonas's finger. "How's that?"

He looked down at his hand and then at Olivia's small clutch purse. "Don't tell me—you also have a justice of the peace in there, right?"

"Cute, Jonas," she said, glaring at him. "Well, I guess we're set." She took him by the arm and steered them through a vast sea of conventioneers.

Jonas glanced down at her skeptically. "Set for what is the question."

"Don't worry, you're doing great," Olivia assured him. "Thanks for coming to my rescue. I promise this won't last too much longer."

"In some absurd way, the whole thing is rather amusing."

"I'm glad somebody's having fun. By the way, think you could lighten up on those cozy hugs a bit?"

"My, aren't we testy! I thought you'd be delighted to have found someone willing to go along with this little charade."

"I'm sorry. Honest." Olivia looked up at him then and he could see that she meant it. She shook her head. "It's just that being with these people after so many years has got me kind of rattled."

"That's okay," he said kindly. "A lot of couples bicker. It doesn't necessarily mean we have a bad marriage."

She looked up to see that he was grinning wryly at her. "Who are Brad and Marsha anyway?" he continued. "I gather that you all know each other from college, but something else is going on here. Want to tell me about it?"

"It's too complicated to explain right now. I'll tell you later," Olivia promised, walking slightly faster.

Jonas gripped her wrist to slow her down; not hard, but not exactly gently, either. "Why don't you try it now, in twenty words or less? I think I have the right to know *something* about what's going on—dearest," he added with exaggerated sweetness.

Olivia slowed her pace and looked down at the floor. "Marsha was my roommate in college and my best friend. Brad, her husband, was my fiancé. Got the picture?"

"I believe so." Jonas was silent for a moment, mulling over the information. Betrayal. He knew something about that all right. His instinct to help this woman had been correct after all. "That's amazing," he said finally.

"What? That my roommate stole my fiancé?"

"No, not that. Pretty lowdown of her, but it probably happens all the time." When she turned to look at him, he was counting something out on his fingers. "I asked you to explain it in twenty words or less and you managed to tell the whole story in that amount exactly."

Olivia caught his glance. His eyes were twinkling now. "By the way, what do you do for a living?" he asked casually. "In case the topic should come up in conversation it would be nice if I knew."

"I'm an actress. Soap operas. Though I'm presently 'in between projects' as we say in the trade. That means I'm looking for work."

"An actress. I might have guessed." He sighed. "You haven't made up some glamour job for me, have you?" he asked cautiously. "Like telling your friend I'm an oil tycoon?"

Olivia turned to him with sudden interest. "Are you?"

"Of course not," he snapped back.

"Well that's not my fault," she said in a slightly injured tone. "I was very vague about what you did for a living. I guess you can tell them whatever you like. What do you really do?"

"I'm in advertising. I used to have a partnership, but now I'm on my own."

"Advertising? Well, that's a start I guess. It should be easy for you to make up something really interesting then."

Jonas stared at her. They had reached the entrance to the restaurant lounge and both caught sight of Marsha and Brad waving from a table in the corner.

"Well, here we go," Olivia said, as she took Jonas's arm.

She was so nervous she could barely put one foot in front of the other. Dealing with Marsha was bad enough, but as they approached the table she realized that she had not really prepared herself for confronting Brad again.

But there was no time to worry about that now. They arrived at the table and a sandy-haired man rose from his seat, smiling at her with his hand outstretched. Olivia was suddenly grateful for the solid, supporting strength of Jonas's arm.

Two

———

Olivia, how good to see you." Brad took her hand and pressed it between both of his. "You look absolutely marvelous."

"Good to see you too, Brad," Olivia said smoothly. She smiled at him, surprised at how easy it was after all. "I'd like you to meet my husband, Jonas," she said, stepping aside so that the two men could shake hands.

She could feel Brad and Jonas sizing each other up, like two prizefighters who had just entered the ring. All in the most polite and civilized manner, of course.

Bradford Carmichael had nothing to be ashamed of, she thought. Time had been more than kind to her old beau. He still had his hair, all of it, which was touched with silver among the sandy blond strands. He was trim and fit. No unsightly spare tire. Olivia sighed. Brad looked better than ever. He definitely looked richer.

"Well, isn't this nice," Marsha said inanely once they were all seated. "Together at last. What luck to have run into you this afternoon, Olivia."

"That was something, wasn't it?"

"I couldn't believe my eyes," Marsha said to Jonas, placing one hand dramatically at the base of her throat. "There she was, out of the clear blue. She hasn't changed a bit, has she, Brad?" she asked, turning to her husband.

Brad, who had been silently staring at Olivia since she arrived, now looked down into his drink and swirled the ice around the bottom of the glass. "No, not a bit. I would recognize you anywhere," he replied, looking briefly but intensely into Olivia's eyes.

The waiter arrived to take their order, saving Olivia the trouble of an appropriate reply.

"So how long have you two been together?" Marsha asked in a tone that suggested she was out for every last dirty detail.

"Six months," Olivia said.

"Two years," Jonas answered at the same time.

Marsha laughed, glancing from one to the other. "Now, I've heard of forgetting one's anniversary, but..."

"We started living together two years ago," Olivia offered as an explanation. "But we only made it official six months ago."

Jonas reached over and took Olivia's hand, lacing his fingers between hers. "Two years, two hours—what's the difference? When I'm with Olivia," he went on poetically, "I forget the meaning of time." He turned and looked lovingly into Olivia's eyes. "I forget the meaning of a lot of things in fact," he added with a small, sly smile.

Olivia felt a warm flood of color creeping up her neck and had to look away.

"Isn't that sweet," Marsha cooed. "True love if I ever saw it."

"Looks like the real thing all right." Brad smiled tightly and sipped his Scotch.

"And how did you two meet?" Marsha continued with her interrogation.

"Uh—well, there's really not much to tell," Olivia said truthfully. Jonas laughed and she glared at him.

"Come on now, Olivia. Don't be shy with us," Marsha coaxed.

"Why don't you let me tell the story, honey?" Jonas offered. "You know it's one of my *favorites*. Especially the part about the touchdown..."

"Touchdown? Oh, you met at a football game?" Marsha asked.

"No...not exactly." Olivia dealt Jonas a glance that was pure poison and promised a slow and painful death if he so much as dared to interrupt her. "Where shall I begin?" she said sweetly, trying to collect her thoughts. She wanted the tale to be romantic, glamorous, the meeting with that perfect man that every woman dreams of. In short, she wanted to see Marsha curdle with envy. "I was in the South of France," she began, with an appropriately dreamy tone to her voice. Jonas winced audibly, and with precise aim she struck his shin with the pointed toe of her shoe beneath the table.

"The South of France? How lovely. Brad and I vacationed there last spring, also."

Leave it to Marsha to reduce this scenario to a mundane vacation pickup, Olivia thought. "Oh, I wasn't on vacation," she corrected. "I had just been at the film festival in Cannes and stopped by to see some friends—a French filmmaker and his wife—who have a château in the area."

"Olivia makes friends easily," Jonas interjected.

"Oh, so mutual friends brought you two together," Marsha surmised. "A blind date perhaps?"

A blind date? How degrading, Olivia thought. No, that explanation would never do. She racked her brain for some image that was a bit more enchanting, but before she could think of anything suitably romantic, Jonas spoke up.

"Oh, it wasn't anything like a blind date. Just an ordinary oil leak," he said with a nonchalant shrug of his shoulders. "One of those rented cars I picked up in Paris. I managed to make it to this château and Olivia answered the door. I never imagined that gasket problems could lead to such delightful consequences," he said with a charming smile.

Olivia could have kicked him again for ruining her romantic buildup with a conclusion as mundane as leaky engine gaskets. But remarkably, it all seemed to have the desired effect on Marsha.

"Oh, how romantic," Marsha said, sighing in a way that told Olivia that their combined efforts had finally hit pay dirt. "I guess you two were just fated to meet and live happily ever after."

"It did seem very...uh, fateful," Olivia agreed. As for "the happily ever after" part, it was certainly much too early in the evening to even take a guess at that.

"I guess that taught you to fool around with those foreign cars," Brad teased Jonas. "Nothing but trouble if you ask me. I'll take a good old Chevy or Buick any day," he expounded, revealing the conservative nature Olivia had always known to be typical of him. "So, what line of work are you in, Jonas?"

"Advertising. I have my own firm—Harper Media."

"I think advertising is just fascinating," Marsha said.

"Some people think so," Jonas replied, glancing sideways at Olivia.

"I've been looking for a good advertising agency for months." Brad shook his head dolefully. "Just can't seem to find anyone with fresh ideas, with energy, with pizzazz. I've just picked up this great new company, too. Multi-Foods...maybe you've heard of them?" he asked, nonchalantly mentioning a name that Olivia knew was a corporate giant. Jonas, who had not taken much interest in Brad so far, suddenly sat up as if he had received an electric shock through the seat of his pants. "We have several product lines you know," Brad continued. "Coffee, cereal, soup, baby food... you name it. But I've been very unhappy with the firm that's handled our TV spots in the past."

"Faber and Wyatt," Jonas said succinctly.

"Why, yes. Well, between you and me," Brad said, lowering his voice to almost a whisper, "those boys are getting the ax. I just haven't found the kind of firm I want to replace them," he said, sighing. "It's a big job."

"That it is," Jonas agreed solemnly.

Jonas looked at Brad. Brad looked at Jonas. There was a moment of complete and utter silence.

"What about Jonas, dear?" Marsha asked quietly. "Maybe he could help you out."

"Maybe I could, Brad," Jonas said in an offhand manner. "I have done some work in this area before." He named some very impressive clients that even caused Olivia to regard him with new respect.

"Well, what do you know. This could be my lucky day. Let's talk about this more later in private, shall we? I'm afraid we might be boring the ladies." Brad smiled at Marsha and Olivia.

"Oh, I'm not the least bit bored," Marsha said brightly. "Tell me, Jonas. Is the competition in New York as vicious as people say?"

"It's worse than they say," he replied. "That's why my firm is in San Diego."

"Your firm is in San Diego? But I thought you two lived in New York," Brad said.

"Uh—we have a New York office, of course," Jonas corrected himself. He turned to Olivia, his eyes pleading for her to bail him out.

"And a house in California. We kind of take turns in each other's home state," she tried to explain, feeling as if she was sinking rapidly into a bed of quicksand.

"Oh, you have one of those *bicoastal* marriages," Marsha said with awe.

"That's it exactly," Olivia said, relieved that someone at the table had come up with the answer. "Jonas and I felt that just because we were getting married, it didn't mean that one of us had to give up their work and their home and their...uh..."

"Coast," Jonas finished for her.

"How enlightened," Marsha said. "Don't you think so, Brad?"

"I might be old-fashioned," Brad said, "but it doesn't sound much like being married to me."

"It doesn't *feel* like being married, either," Jonas remarked in a thoughtful tone.

Damn him, Olivia thought frantically. He's going to blow the whole thing. I've seen that suspicious look in Marsha's eye before. "Well, I certainly feel married," she said, sliding next to Jonas on the bench seat and laying her arm across his shoulder. She toyed playfully with the small dark curls at the back of his neck that just touched his collar. "As a matter of fact, I'm out here now, looking for a role that will let us have more time together," she explained in a voice full of suppressed longing.

"Well, it must be difficult to be apart for long periods of time," Marsha said sympathetically. "Especially since you're relatively newlyweds."

"Yes, it's hard to be apart," Olivia agreed. "But it's so much fun when we get back together again, if you know what I mean." Olivia, who had remained cuddled up to Jonas, petting him in an absentminded way, noticed suddenly that her feigned attentions were having a very real effect on the man. His skin was getting warm to her touch, and his hands, which rested in his lap, were gripped into white-knuckled fists.

"So you're still acting then, Olivia?" Brad asked.

"Of course she's acting," Jonas said tightly. "This woman deserves an Academy Award, from what I've seen."

"Oh, honey, you have to stop that," Olivia scolded sweetly. "He's always bragging about me," she said with a sigh. "It's positively embarrassing."

"Nonsense, he's just proud of you," Brad said. "He knows what a lucky guy he is."

"Believe me, Brad. Luck had nothing to do with it," Jonas replied in a soft but menacing tone. He reached up behind his neck and removed Olivia's teasing fingers, but did not let go of her hand. His grip was like iron and the look in his eyes made her feel that perhaps she had gone a bit too far. "Let's dance, dear," he said in a deep, controlled voice.

Olivia took one look at his forbidding expression and felt her mouth grow dry. "Uh—I really don't feel like dancing right now, honey." Frankly, she was terrified of being alone with him.

"Of course you do, sweetheart." He stood, yanking her up with him in a way that gave her no choice but to stand. He smiled politely at Brad and Marsha. "You'll excuse us for a moment, won't you?" he asked, all but shoving Olivia out in front of him.

"Of course. Have fun," Brad said. "When you get back, we'll order dinner."

"Dinner?" Olivia squeaked. "Oh, I don't think we can possibly..."

"We'd be delighted to have dinner with you," Jonas cut in. He wrapped one arm around Olivia's waist and literally swept her away from the table. "Be right back," he promised.

Out on the dance floor Jonas glared down at her without saying a word. She placed one hand lightly on his shoulder, and stood some distance away from him, conscious of the heavy masculine hand that rested possessively on her hip. "Come over here," he said, pulling her closer. He wrapped both arms around her in such an intimate embrace that she couldn't help placing both her hands against his broad chest. "We're still on our honeymoon, remember? You can't dance with me as if we were at a church social."

For once he had her at a loss for words. She was totally distracted by Jonas's nearness, the sensation of their bodies touching from head to toe. She had to admit that it was a very pleasant feeling. It felt so natural to be held close by this man. But somehow, in the back of her mind, she had suspected it would be like this.

For such a large man, he was surprisingly light on his feet. It was easy to follow his lead as they moved out onto the floor among the other couples. "Relax a little, would you?" Jonas whispered into her ear. He placed his fingertips at her nape and lightly massaged the knotted muscles there. Olivia closed her eyes and savored the sensation. She hadn't realized how tense she was until now. This whole ordeal was exhausting and she couldn't wait until it was over. Very soon she felt herself turning her cheek into Jonas's shoulder, her head fitting neatly below his chin.

"That's better," Jonas said. "I wouldn't worry about a thing. They actually believe this ridiculous charade."

"Mission accomplished," she murmured, lifting her head slightly. "After this dance, we'll say our goodnights and go our separate ways. No sense in pushing our luck. You've been great, Jonas," she added as an afterthought. "I don't know how to thank you."

"The evening's not over quite yet. You owe me," he said simply.

"Meaning what?" She pulled away from him and looked up at the determined expression on his face. It did not bode well, she thought. He had done her a tremendous favor, that was true. But what exactly did this man expect as fair payment for services rendered?

He laughed then and she had the distinct feeling he had read her mind. "I think you've misunderstood me, dear Olivia."

"Have I?"

"If you think I'm planning to follow you up to
room and continue playing my role...out of
tume, so to speak..."

"Well, that's a relief!"

"Is it really?" He sounded genuinely insulte
wouldn't have thought so from the way you cu
up next to me at the table a few minutes ago."

"That was just part of the act," she said light
part she had very much enjoyed, she neglected to
"I apologize if it...bothered you, Jonas."

"I don't think 'bothered' is exactly the wo
would have used. But let me say this, try that pa
the act again, Olivia, and I will pull you under tl
ble and give both Marsha and Brad a very convir
show of conjugal bliss. Do you get my meaning?

"You're coming in loud and clear," she respo
tersely.

"Good. Now, as I was saying about repayin
favor, your old sweetheart, Brad, has hinted at a
tastically juicy business opportunity. Landing
Multi-Foods account is an ad man's equivaler
winning the lottery," he explained, guiding
smoothly across the dance floor. "A man could i
after signing that account."

She knew what he was driving at, but hor
wished that she didn't. "You're hardly old enou,
worry about retiring, Jonas. You've got years to
it out," she assured him.

"That's not the point, Olivia," he said in de
earnest.

"The point is that you want to stay for dinner, right?" She tilted her head back and peered up at him.

He nodded with a thin smile. "Dinner and whatever else it takes to get this account."

"I don't know, Jonas," Olivia said nervously. "I just have this awful feeling that the longer we stay with them, the easier it'll be for them to guess that we're not really married." She glanced up at him briefly, hoping that she was gaining some ground. It was impossible to read the expression on his face. "I'm not even worrying about myself now, Jonas. Honest. If Brad finds out that we've been fooling them all evening, he'll never trust you with his advertising, will he?" she said, trying to appeal to his sense of logic.

"We'll just have to keep them from guessing then, won't we?" he said with infuriating calm. "The trouble is that we've been letting Marsha do all the talking. I feel like I'm being interrogated by a senate committee, for heaven's sake."

"Well what do you suggest?" Olivia could feel her temper rising. "That we plead the Fifth?"

"Just start asking her some questions. Get them talking about their kids and their pets—I don't know. Whatever people like her like to brag about."

"I don't give a damn about their kids and their pets," Olivia replied in a low growl. "This is not going to work for an entire evening. You're going to have to figure some other way to retire before you're forty. How about the stock market? Or real estate?"

"You didn't think this was so impossible about an hour ago, when you strutted up to me in that bar."

"Strutted?" she repeated in disbelief.

"Yes, strutted, my dear. As in 'to strut one's stuff,'" he replied, explaining the term in a low, angry voice.

"That was different," she argued. "I was desperate and probably temporarily insane." She looked up at his stern expression and could tell that he remained unconvinced. "It's a miracle that we've gotten this far."

"I'll agree to that," he spit out, "and to the admission of insanity, though from what I've seen I'm not sure I would diagnose it as a temporary condition. A château in the south of France? That was pushing it, don't you think?"

"Why did you have to say that your firm was based in California when you know I told them that we lived in New York?" she challenged him. "That didn't exactly help matters either."

"Quiet down, will you?" He glanced quickly over his shoulder. "They're looking at us, I think." He pulled her close again and nuzzled his cheek against her temple in a very convincing show of husbandly affection.

Olivia felt so angry she thought she was going to burst. But at the same time, in spite of herself, she could feel her body responding again to Jonas's nearness. The hard, lean planes of his chest pressed against the soft contours of her breasts. The scent of his skin and the feeling of his breath stirring the loose wisps of hair by her cheek made her shiver.

"Let's not blow our cover altogether," he whispered in her ear. "That won't do either of us any good, will it?"

She sighed. "I guess you're right," she admitted grudgingly.

"I hate to put it to you this way, Olivia, but you're dealing with a desperate man. If you don't agree to help me out, now that the shoe is on the other foot, I'm going to do something you won't like."

"Such as?" Her head, which had been resting on his shoulder, suddenly popped up.

"I'll walk back to the table right now and tell them everything."

"You wouldn't!" Olivia stopped dancing and just looked up at him.

"Try me," he replied simply. His dark face was an expressionless mask. His eyes, which she had seen sparkle so warmly from time to time throughout the evening, now gazed down at her icily.

Olivia ran her tongue over her dry lips and considered her choices. The fact was she really didn't have any. Besides, in her heart she knew that Jonas was right. She did owe him for doing her the favor to begin with. It was just that he had chosen such an awfully unfortunate form of repayment.

"You drive a hard bargain," she said finally.

"Does that mean you agree to my request?"

She reluctantly nodded. "I suppose I can survive staying married to you through dinner."

"Thanks," he said dryly. "You certainly do wonders for a man's ego, Olivia."

"I mean, after all, I did get you into this mess. The least I can do is help you get a little something out of it."

"I knew you'd begin to see it my way." The music had picked up in pace and he swirled her gracefully toward the center of the dance floor. "I don't know why people find it so difficult to stay married," he said. "You see how easy it is to work out our differences if we just talk things over?"

"Thank you, 'Dear Abby,'" Olivia replied tartly. "You seem to be forgetting your little ultimatum."

He smiled predatorialy. "Admit it, Olivia. Your conscience would have bothered you for weeks if you hadn't agreed to help me. I was just trying to help you do the right thing."

She looked into his laughing eyes briefly, and then turned away. He did have an uncanny knack for reading her mind, even though they barely knew each other. "A few hours, *maybe* ... not weeks. And don't you dare get smug on me, Jonas," she warned him. "I can't stomach gloaters."

"Me? Gloat?" he said innocently. "I wouldn't dream of it."

"We're going back to the table to eat our dinner and that is it. That's our deal," she finished emphatically.

"You have my solemn word," he promised.

"You'd better chew fast," she warned him, "and no dessert."

"I never touch sweets," he said earnestly. His glance dropped to the low-cut neckline of her dress and lingered there a moment. "The kind that are served with a knife and fork, that is," he added, looking back up at her with mischief in his eyes.

"Don't push your luck."

The music stopped, but his arms remained around her in a loose embrace. He smiled down at her smugly. "You're gorgeous when you're backed into a corner."

She sighed, pulling away. "Let's just get this over with, shall we?" She took his arm and led him toward the table, not wanting to acknowledge the powerful effect he seemed to have over her.

Three

Three

———

You are a liar and I refuse to allow you to step one foot inside this room.'' Olivia stood at the door to her hotel room, her arms folded across her chest, her key in one hand.

"Olivia, just try to control yourself for a minute, will you?'' Jonas pleaded. He ran his hand nervously through his thick, dark hair. "Let's not stand out in the hallway arguing like this.''

"Fine with me. I'm going to take something for my indigestion—like arsenic maybe—and go to bed,'' she said, fitting her key into the lock. "So long, Jonas.'' She stepped through the door and began to close it in his face.

"You're not being reasonable," he said, sticking his foot in the crack between the door and the doorframe. He wrapped one hand around the knob and leaned his full weight against the door. "Just tell me what I did that was so awful and I promise I'll leave you alone."

"Tell you what you did?" She turned on him furiously. "You know what you did. You invited Brad and Marsha to spend the weekend at our beach house. That's what you *did*."

Jonas winced. "Aside from that," he said meekly.

"Aside from that? How about doing everything in your power to make that dinner drag on for hours? You ordered a lobster that had to be brought out of the kitchen on a fork lift and you sent back that Caesar salad no less than three times," she reminded him with merciless accuracy. "Not to mention the dessert, which required a team of waiters to prepare at our table and a team of busboys to come and put out the centerpiece flambé."

"Now you can hardly blame me for that, Olivia. We were lucky they had enough fire extinguishers on hand."

"Which didn't stop you from throwing yourself across Marsha as if you were trying to wrestle her to the ground or something," she bit out tersely.

"I thought I saw a few sparks fly onto her dress. I was only trying to help. I think you're just jealous."

"Jealous? Ha! That's a laugh," she shouted, opening the door wider than she meant to.

Jonas seized the chance to wiggle past her and step inside the room.

"I told you I didn't want you in here," she said, turning to confront him.

"I heard you. So did most of the other guests in this hotel." He reached over her shoulder and pushed the door closed. "We're going to sit down and talk this out like two rational, mature adults."

Olivia quickly walked toward the telephone that sat on a small writing desk near the window. "I'm going to count to three, Jonas. If you don't get out of here, you'll be discussing your problems with two rational, mature security guards."

"Put that phone down, Olivia," Jonas warned, coming toward her.

"I will not." She glanced at him over her shoulder. He was one angry-looking man. Her finger shook slightly as she began to punch the appropriate extension.

Without a word, he leaned over, wrapped his hand around the cord that led from the phone to the wall and gave a sharp tug. Olivia held the receiver to her ear just in time to hear the line go dead.

She slammed the receiver down and turned to look at Jonas, who had stepped back a few feet and was standing calmly, with his arms folded across his chest. "That does it. I've had just about all I'm going to take from you, Jonas." Picking up the entire phone with two hands she hurled it at his head.

Jonas ducked. The projectile whizzed over his head and crashed into the wall behind him with a plaintive chime. Cautiously he stood up again and looked over at her. "I suppose you know that the hotel is going to charge you for that," he said smugly. "I hope it was fun."

"Frankly, it would have been a lot *more* fun if I had hit you with it." She pushed back a lock of hair that had fallen across her eyes. The sudden expenditure of anger, not to mention the fact that it was nearly two o'clock in the morning, had exhausted her. Olivia sat down heavily on the edge of the bed with a disgusted sigh. "What a night," she muttered to herself.

Jonas remained standing. He had removed his jacket and tie, which he folded neatly and hung over the back of a chair. He looked down at her calmly as he unfastened the top buttons of his collar. "Are you ready to talk this over now?" he asked calmly.

"It doesn't look as if I have any choice in the matter, does it?"

"I know what I did tonight seems somewhat..." His voice trailed off as he searched for a word that would not be totally self-incriminating.

"Unscrupulous?" Olivia offered. "Conniving? Unconscionable?"

"Okay." He held up his hands in a sign of surrender. "I've got your point. I know I promised that we'd only have dinner with the Carmichaels and then go our separate ways...."

"A *quick* dinner," she reminded him. "You even promised to chew fast."

"I remember what I promised, Olivia," he replied with the utmost restraint over his temper.

"Sure you do, now, when it's convenient. What happened down in the restaurant? Things were working out just as you wanted, Jonas. Brad even offered to see you when he got back to San Francisco and discuss your ideas. During regular business hours," she added, her temper beginning to rise once more. "I don't know why that wasn't good enough for you."

"Believe me, Olivia," he replied, pacing back and forth before her as if he were a trial attorney pleading a case, "it just wouldn't be the same as having an entire weekend to persuade him in a secluded, relaxing atmosphere like my beach house."

"Our beach house," she corrected. "You even promised that I would whip up some of my fantastic paella, for heaven's sake. I don't know the first thing about making paella. Fantastic or otherwise. If it doesn't come in a box that says micro-wavable on the front, it's really not in my repertoire," she finished tartly.

"Paella is a very simple dish to prepare," he explained patiently, "and guests adore it. I'll make it but we can say you did."

"That's not the point," she said, slamming her hand down on the bed.

Jonas stopped pacing for a moment and rubbed his jaw with his hand, staring down thoughtfully at a spot on the rug. "Olivia, before we start fighting again, just give me a minute to explain something to you. Maybe after I'm through you'll see this situation a bit differently." His tone was one of quiet appeal. She could tell that whatever he had to say, it was going to be difficult for him.

"All right," she said, her temper reined. "I'm listening."

"I honestly don't know why I decided to help you out at first, but when you told me that story about you, Marsha and Brad, I was glad that I did. I not only sympathize with how it feels to be betrayed by the two people closest to you, I've gone through it myself."

"Tell me about it," she said quietly.

"My partner, my best friend throughout college—because I trusted him so completely he was able to steal our firm right out from under my nose. He walked off with all our major accounts—including a cosmetics firm represented by a woman executive I idiotically believed was in love with me," he said grimly.

"How awful," she said, her anger suddenly dispelled and replaced by genuine sympathy.

"My 'friend' has all but ruined my professional reputation, taking credit for his work and mine, too. In spite of that, I've done fairly well the past year or so, getting my own agency off the ground. We have some big accounts but nothing like Multi-Foods. Brad even mentioned that my ex-partner's agency is romancing him for the contract. He's supposed to meet with them next week up in San Francisco for a final presentation." He rubbed his hands over his face, suddenly looking tired and worn out. "This weekend might be my only chance to make a play for this account, Olivia. It would sure mean a lot to me if I got it.''

Jonas stopped pacing and looked deeply into her eyes. She felt like judge and jury rolled into one. He looked as strong and indomitable as he had first appeared in the bar, yet she now perceived a certain vulnerability to his character that she had not sensed before. Just by looking at him—the somber expression on his lean face, his powerful shoulders and the V-shaped patch of dark hair revealed by his open shirt collar—she again felt the stirrings of desire for him.

She didn't know whether she was willing to agree to this latest scheme. She only knew she ached to walk over to where he stood, wrap her arms around him and tell him to worry about the rest of it in the morning. Tomorrow he could probably talk her into anything he liked; that was just the problem, she thought, fighting off the urge to make a move toward him.

"I—I'm really quite confused, Jonas," she said finally, pulling her gaze away from his. "My feet ache so much, I can't even see straight." She pulled off one shoe and tossed it disgustedly on the rug.

"I'll never understand why women wear those things if they hurt so much."

"To *strut our stuff*, naturally," she replied, easing her swollen foot out of the other shoe. "You know what they say, Jonas: 'no pain, no gain.'"

Jonas leaned over and picked up a discarded high-heeled shoe. "Who designed these things? The Marquis de Sade?"

"I wouldn't be surprised. Oh, Lord, I'll never dance again," she moaned as she rubbed one foot with her hand. "It was a man for sure, anyway."

Jonas watched her for a moment. "That's not the way to do it properly." Kneeling down on the rug, he took her foot into his strong hands. "Here, let me," he offered as he began rotating his thumbs from the base of her heel to the tip of her toes with a smooth, penetrating touch. Nerve endings tingled from her toenails to her spine and back again. "How does that feel?" he inquired after a few moments.

"Heavenly," she sighed.

"Madam," he said, taking her other foot in his hands, "you haven't felt anything close to heaven yet."

Olivia looked down at him, vaguely alerted by the deep, seductive quality of his tone. He was intent on his task, his dark head bowed, his hands methodically working their magic, easing up her ankle and calf at a rate that was deliciously unhurried. She closed her eyes, surrendering herself to the experience of Jonas's nimble fingers as they languorously massaged their way up the length of her long, lean legs. Resting back on the bed, Olivia couldn't think of one good reason to ask him to stop. She felt as if her brain was becoming anesthetized by the sensations his touch had elicited.

Suddenly, she became aware that he had stopped. She slowly opened her eyes and sat up, to find him kneeling directly in front of her, his face inches from her own, his hands resting on either side of her thighs.

Close up like this, his eyes looked dark green with occasional flashes of amber light.

"Feel better now?" he asked her.

She nodded and said nothing, studying the shape of his mouth. Without thinking, she lifted her hand and outlined the shape of his lower lip with her fingertip. "Now it's your turn," she said, winding her arms around his neck.

She could feel a shudder move through his big body as he leaned toward her. "Olivia," he sighed, his hands sliding up the silk fabric that covered her thighs as his lips met hers in a hungry kiss. Olivia gripped his shoulders, their mouths never parting as he rose up and sat next to her on the bed. Olivia leaned back and Jonas followed, his kiss deepening as he eased down on top of her. Olivia's fingers curled into his thick dark hair and she stretched out beneath him. As his mouth pressed against hers, she felt as if the very breath was being drawn out of her.

Somewhere in the back of her mind, she realized that she had been wondering all night what this would feel like. Now she knew for sure—total devastation, total intoxication. She couldn't remember ever wanting to be close to anyone the way she now wanted to be close to Jonas. His mouth moved from hers to cover her face and neck with hot, adoring kisses. His hands swept up from her thighs, across her hips and ribs cage to cup her breasts, lightly moving over them until she shuddered with pleasure.

Olivia sighed, pulling his head back toward hers, her mouth seeking out his kiss. Her tongue twined and twirled deliciously with his as her hands massaged the hard ridge of muscle on his shoulders.

"That feels so good." He lifted his head, sighing with pleasure as his hand tangled gently in her hair. "You feel like heaven in my arms, Olivia. I can't wait until we're alone together out at the house. Just think—we'll have all day and night tomorrow before the Carmichaels arrive Saturday."

"The beach house?" Olivia lifted her head and suddenly sat up, feeling as if she had been doused with a bucket of cold water. "Who said anything about going to any beach house with you, Jonas? I certainly never did." The more she considered the implications, the angrier she became. "Or is that what this is really all about?"

Jonas pushed himself up on his elbows, his expression one of bewilderment. "Where are you going?" he demanded as she slid away from him and off the bed.

"Not with you, that's for sure. Not today, tomorrow or ever." She pushed up the thin straps of her dress and smoothed the skirt back down around her knees. "You thought if you could get me into bed tonight, I'd agree to play house for the weekend, didn't you?"

"Of course not. That's not what I thought at all." He sat up on the edge of the bed and ran his hand wearily through his hair.

"You've already lied to me once tonight, Jonas," she said, pacing restlessly around the room. "I'm not buying this time."

"How could you say that?" He bounded off the bed and came toward her. "What we both felt," he said, gesturing toward the bed, "that was the *real* thing, Olivia. Not another scene from our little act downstairs. At least, for *me* it wasn't."

He searched out her gaze, trying to read her expression. She looked briefly into his eyes and then away, crossing her arms tightly over her chest. "About going out to Newport Beach," he continued a bit more hesitantly, "I only thought that—"

"Well, you thought wrong," she cut in. She knew if she allowed him to keep talking he would break down her resolve. "It's very late, Jonas. I want you to go."

"All right, if that's what you want." He stared at her a long moment, then tucked in his shirt and stepped into his shoes. "I don't need to be told twice."

Walking over to where she stood he picked up his jacket and tie from the armchair. "I'll see you later, Olivia," he promised as he walked toward the door. He paused for a moment before stepping out into the hallway. "You know it's very easy to draw people into your life," he said, glancing at her over his shoulder. "But, for better or worse, it's not quite as easy to get rid of them."

She stared at his back as he walked out and quietly closed the door behind him. "And where did you pick up that little tidbit of wisdom, Mr. Madison Avenue? A fortune cookie, maybe?"

Olivia let the hot water in the shower beat down on her back for a long time. Still, once she was under the covers, she could not seem to relax, though she longed for sleep. Random thoughts and images of the strange evening that had just passed filled her head—thoughts of Marsha, Brad and Jonas. Mostly, she had to admit, of Jonas. From the minute she spotted him, she should have known he was going to be trouble with a capital *T*. Olivia punched her pillows and flopped over on her side.

Arguing with the man seemed pointless. He had the most uncanny knack of getting around her. Olivia had never experienced anything quite like it. And that went double for the experience of kissing him. The thought rushed unbidden into her mind. Olivia stretched out on her back again and stared up at the ceiling. So, big deal, she answered herself, so the man possesses one redeeming quality. That hardly outweighs about a dozen other traits I consider totally unacceptable. Pulling the blankets up around her chin, she tried to get comfortable again. Sure, he's got a few rough edges that need polishing, a mischievous inner voice murmured. Nothing the right woman couldn't handle—nothing that she wouldn't consider a challenge, in fact. As for weighing the undesirable traits against the more…desirable, are we talking quality right now, Olivia? Or just quantity?

Her thoughts continued to seesaw as she turned and twisted. Sleep finally came shortly before dawn.

Olivia's dreams were vivid. She saw herself shooting a scene on the familiar set of the soap opera, *All Our Tomorrows*. Jonas was once again holding her, kissing her, thrilling her with his every touch. Then

Marsha swept into the room. "So you're not really married after all," she accused them dramatically. "I should have known. Married people don't kiss like *that*!"

"Cut! Cut!" the director shouted. Olivia looked up to find that it was Jonas again, in the director's chair this time. "That's not the way it's supposed to go at all. Can't you people get your blasted lines straight?" he railed. "Amateurs! A bunch of amateurs!"

Olivia sat up with a start. The sound of her own voice, shouting back at Jonas had awakened her. It took her a moment to get her breath and realize where she was. The digital clock on the bedside table read 5:32 in glowing green numbers. Her mind surprisingly clear, she leaned back against the pillows and considered her situation. She felt as if she was the only soul awake in the whole hotel. Of course, in a few short hours she would have more company than she wanted. Not only would she have Marsha and Brad to contend with, there would also be Jonas.

Olivia sighed. For the life of her, she couldn't seem to recall why proving herself to Marsha had been so terribly important. At this point, she honestly didn't give a hoot what the Carmichaels thought of her. Purely by chance, she had managed to avoid them for ten years. Surely, with just the slightest bit of forethought, she could manage to stay out of their path for another twenty. As for Jonas Harper, any woman with an IQ higher than that of a houseplant could see that the man would simply cause more problems than he was worth. Realizing she tended to be attracted to the wrong kind of man, Olivia thought she would nip the situation in the bud for once. Putting distance between herself and the smooth-talking advertising whiz would be the best favor she had done herself in a long time.

While Jonas and the Carmichaels slept soundly in their beds, Olivia decided that she would dress, pack and check out of the hotel. It was the coward's way out to be sure, but the only logical solution to her dilemma. Having finally caught sight of a light at the end of the tunnel, Olivia bounded out of bed with renewed energy. Last evening had been a ridiculous episode and one of her own making. But it would all be over soon, she assured herself as she ran from the closet to the open suitcase on her bed, hastily tossing in armfuls of clothing.

Barely a half hour later, Olivia was standing beside her luggage at the front desk in the hotel lobby. With the exception of a few of the hotel's personnel, the area was deserted. The perfect time to make my escape, Olivia thought with secret glee as she handed her credit card to the desk clerk. She would take a cab to the airport and then book herself on the first available flight to L.A. By the time anyone woke up and discovered that she was gone, she would be sipping her morning dose of black coffee at an altitude of thirty thousand feet. Olivia signed her bill with a flourish, secretly congratulating herself for a job well done.

"Do you need any help with your bags, ma'am?"

"I think I can manage," Olivia assured the clerk. She had piled up her few pieces of luggage behind her, balanced against a chair. Not so far away that she couldn't reach them in a few quick steps, but not so close that she would be in danger of falling down backward over them, either. Now when she turned to look at them, she discovered that they were gone. Olivia was stunned for a moment. "My bags—they've disappeared," she finally exclaimed.

"Gone, ma'am? Are you sure?"

"Of course I'm sure. They were right over there—a hanging bag, an overnight case and one of those carryon pieces. Red canvas. Right there," she repeated, pointing this time.

"Well..." the desk clerk said slowly. He was no more than twenty, Olivia guessed, blue-eyed and blond, with that sunstruck, laid-back manner Olivia found typical of Southern Californians. "Gee—I can't imagine somebody just walking off with them. This isn't New York City, ma'am," he reminded her with a grin.

"No argument there," Olivia assured him.

"Well—maybe one of the bellmen took them out front by mistake. Let me check on that," he said, picking up a phone. Olivia nervously drummed her fingers on the countertop. Finally he looked up at her and shrugged. "No answer out there. Why don't you just step outside and take a look around? If you don't see them, you come directly back. I'll be right here."

"Now there's a comforting thought for you," Olivia muttered as she headed for the revolving door.

Out in front of the hotel, Olivia's gaze quickly swept the sidewalk. Not a red canvas bag in sight. Not even a bellhop. She squinted against the early-morning sun, automatically pulling down the big, wraparound-style sunglasses that were on top of her head. Seemingly from out of nowhere, a cream-colored Mercedes 450SL roared up to the curb and screeched to a halt barely inches away from her. The trunk magically opened with a loud pop, and within, Olivia saw her luggage...or at least three red canvas pieces that very much resembled her luggage.

The door opened on the driver's side and Jonas emerged. "Looking for these?" He walked around the car toward her.

"I might have guessed," she said, her hands on her hips.

"Did you really think they were stolen?" He shook his head in a thoroughly irritating know-it-all way. "This isn't Manhattan, Olivia."

"I've been reminded of that once already, thank you. You certainly have a flair for the dramatic, Jonas. I'll grant you that much."

"Well, I consider that quite a compliment, you being in the business and all." He leaned casually against the rear fender, folding his arms loosely across his chest. "I thought it would be an interesting twist to your sneaky little exit scene. The dark glasses are a nice touch, Olivia. Very... incognito."

"Incognito," she repeated angrily. "I'll give you incognito, you insufferable, son of a..." Olivia took a deep breath and regained control of her temper. "I'm going to count to ten. If those bags aren't out of your trunk and on this sidewalk, I'm going to tell the desk clerk that you stole them.''

"What are you getting so excited about?" he asked innocently. "I get up at the crack of dawn to drive you to the airport and this is the thanks I get?"

"Drive me to the airport?" Olivia stared at him suspiciously. He returned her look with a guileless, utterly charming smile. "I can take a cab, thanks." She knew better by now than to trust this man. "My bags, please."

"Whatever you say." He raised his hands in a gesture of surrender and walked to the back of the car. "I just can't understand why you would want to pay good money to sit in the back of some dirty, stuffy cab when you can ride with me, for free, in air-conditioned comfort."

She shrugged. "You can lead a horse to water, but you can't make it drink."

"To say nothing of a mule," he added dryly. He rested his hands on the bags, but made no motion to lift them out, Olivia noticed. "Listen, Olivia, I'm sorry about last night. Really sorry, and I'm just trying to do you a small favor to make up for my behavior. Is that so awful?"

She couldn't stand it when he looked at her like that. Feeling her firm resolve getting soft around the edges Olivia looked up at the sky, as if some divine hand had written a few lines of dialogue up there for her. Not a word. Not a cab in sight, either, she noticed. It was growing warmer by the minute, too. She might have to wait some time before a taxi came, even if she telephoned.

Jonas just watched her, that appealing expression still on his face. He hadn't moved a muscle, had barely breathed, in fact. She sighed. "Well, I guess if you're going in that direction anyway. No sense standing out here arguing about it all morning."

"My point exactly." Before she had time to change her mind he had slammed the hood of the trunk and was standing beside her, opening the car door with a courtly flourish.

Still not convinced she was doing the right thing, Olivia got inside and closed the door. Jonas graced her with a dazzling smile as he started the engine and pulled away from the curb. She did not smile back, but turned her head and stared out the window. He certainly looked happy—*too* happy, she thought suspiciously.

They drove along in complete silence, Jonas deftly maneuvering the sports car through the sparse, early-morning traffic. He had chosen an avenue that ran along the waterfront and Olivia was thankful for the distraction. Just because he had insisted on taking her to the airport didn't mean she had to make a lot of pleasant chitchat on the way. She didn't plan on making any conversation in fact, pleasant or otherwise.

Jonas didn't seem to notice her uncharacteristic reticence. Or, if he had, he didn't deem it worthy of comment. He switched on the radio, tuning from one end of the dial to the other. Rock to classical, all news to call-in, he just couldn't seem to find a station to his liking. The entire business was beginning to get on Olivia's nerves. She was about to say something and then wondered if he was doing it on purpose, just to get her attention. If he was, she wouldn't give him the satisfaction. Instead, she unconsciously bit on her lower lip, trying to ignore the onslaught of erratic, discordant sounds.

Miraculously, moments later, he finally fixed on something. Opera, of all possible choices. Not that Olivia disliked opera, but it wasn't exactly the kind of music she would choose after a sleepless night and before a cup of coffee.

"Now there's some real music for you," Jonas said, turning it up louder. Even in her ragged mental state, Olivia recognized the "Wild Bird" aria from *Carmen*.

"Ta-tum-tum-tum, dee-dum-dum-dum." Suddenly, Jonas joined in, singing along in a full, resonant bass, one hand on the steering wheel, the other conducting an imaginary orchestra. "I don't agree with Carmen's philosophy, however," he said thoughtfully, interrupting his performance, "I mean I don't think real love is like a wild bird, here today, gone tomorrow."

Olivia pressed her hand to her forehead. What had she done to deserve this? Now he was gearing up for a philosophical discussion. "Well, you're not alone, Jonas. As I recall, her jilted boyfriend didn't buy that line, either."

"To put it mildly. But what do you think, Olivia? Do you think love is like a wild bird?" He glanced over at her, an engagingly wistful smile on his hand-some face.

The question seemed straightforward enough, but something warned her about getting involved in a dis-cussion with Jonas that even remotely touched upon this subject. "I think," she said finally, "that I need a cup of coffee and two aspirin before I can give you the kind of answer you really deserve."

"Coffee? Why didn't you say you wanted some coffee? There are a million places to stop along here," he said, seeming totally oblivious of the note of irri-tation in her tone. He leaned over and snapped off the radio. "We don't have to listen to that if you've got a headache. Take a look in the glove compartment for some aspirin."

"Thanks," she said meekly. She opened the glove compartment and extracted a small tin of headache tablets. Now she felt guilty for being such a shrew. There was just no winning with this man. The sooner he dropped her off at the airport the better, she thought.

Olivia had assumed Jonas would pull up to a drive-through window at one of the many fast-food places along the way. But instead, he stopped the car in front of a small dockside café that had tables set up be-neath a yellow-and-white-striped awning outside.

"They have wonderful cappuccino here and these great flaky morning rolls, just like you'd find in Paris." His unflagging good spirits seemed inexhaus-tible this morning. Olivia stared at him in amazement. He couldn't have gotten much more sleep than she had. "You aren't in any special hurry, are you?" he went on. "I mean, is somebody meeting your flight in Los Angeles, or anything like that?"

"I really don't have any appointments until next week." Now why had she admitted that? She could just as easily have told him that she was in a hurry. She suddenly had a premonition that lying would have been the wiser course of action.

"Next week? That's great," he said, bounding out of the car. "We can take our time then."

"Well, I did want to get there sometime during this century," she mumbled to herself.

"What was that, Olivia?"

"Nothing. Nothing at all." She closed the car door and walked beside him to the café entrance. It really was a very pretty spot for breakfast and she could already feel the fresh sea breeze working wonders on her headache.

A few minutes later they were seated at a table with a full view of the harbor. Mugs of frothy, cinnamon-topped cappuccino were in front of them, with a basket of flaky rolls and croissants with individual servings of butter and preserves alongside.

"Now isn't this better than drinking some awful sludge out of a Styrofoam cup at the airport?"

Olivia nodded, and took another sip of her cappuccino.

"This is shaping up to be quite a day. Not a cloud in the sky. I can't understand why you're in such a hurry to get to Los Angeles. Especially since you really don't need to be there until next week. That smog up there will kill you."

So that's what this gourmet breakfast and good cheer was leading up to. Olivia set down her china mug and looked at Jonas. "You forget, Jonas, I was brought up on smog. In fact, too much fresh air makes me light-headed."

"Come on now, Olivia. You can't possibly still be annoyed about last night. Why, you never even gave me a chance to explain. I really think you owe me that much."

She honestly didn't think she owed him anything. But if she refused to let him have his say, he would probably do something crazy, like hold her luggage hostage again until she gave in. "It doesn't look like I have much choice in the matter. Why don't you just say what's on your mind and we'll continue on our merry way to the airport."

"That's just the point. I don't want to take you to the airport at all. At least not today I don't."

"Here we go again." Olivia winced. She could feel her headache return in full force.

"Now before you jump down my throat, just let me make something clear. My interest in you has absolutely nothing to do with Brad Carmichael or the Multi-Foods account, or any of that nonsense," he said emphatically.

"Oh, you mean that nonsense you were planning to retire on last night? Is that the bit of nonsense you're referring to?"

He stared at her solemnly for a moment. But instead of coming back at her with some sarcastic retort, as she expected, he just smiled. Then he shook his head and laughed. "I guess I deserved that…and you are a pro at dishing it out, my dear, I must say." He shrugged. "But maybe that's part of the reason I like you so much. I certainly keep coming back for more," he added, sounding a bit bewildered himself at the whole phenomenon.

His smile was warm and affectionate, causing Olivia to recall the moments last night when it was genuinely delightful pretending to be married to him. Then she caught herself. If she kept thinking in this direction, she'd soon be agreeing to anything he suggested. She dabbed at her mouth with a napkin, then set it beside her plate. "I don't know what this conversation is building up to, Jonas. But I think we'd better drop it right here."

She raised her hand to signal the waiter, but Jonas reached up and pulled it down. "Not so fast," he said, continuing to hold her hand, which was now resting on the tabletop. "You're attracted to me too, Olivia. Admit it. That's what's making you so uncomfortable all of a sudden. Heck, you really can't deny it. With a bar full of men to choose from, you picked me, remember?"

She shook her head in dismay. "And I've been regretting it ever since."

"You don't really mean that. I know you don't." He squeezed her hand and managed to catch her glance with his own. Why in the world did he have to be damnably good-looking? "But if we don't give ourselves a chance to get to know each other better, I know we'll both regret it. In fact, I'm sure of it. Just give it a chance, Olivia. One day, that's all I'm asking. If you're still so dead set on getting to L.A. tomorrow, I'll drive you to the airport first thing in the morning. Besides," he added, toying with her fingers, "you look kind of beat. A relaxing day in the sun would do you good."

He was right about that much. The lack of sleep was really catching up with her. Facing the hustle and bustle at L.A. airport was the last thing Olivia was in the mood for. She wasn't sure if she believed that there was no ulterior motive behind his interest, although they certainly did share a strong attraction to each other. She would rather die, however, than give him the satisfaction of admitting it.

"Frankly, I think you owe me a relaxing day in the sun, just to make up for all the aggravation you caused last night.

"Well, I'm sorry that all you seem to remember is that part of the evening," he said, looking down at his plate. "Does that mean you're agreeing to come with me, or what?" he asked, looking up again.

"No...I mean, ye— Oh, I don't know." Totally confused, she stood up and went over to a wooden railing that overlooked the water.

Jonas was standing beside her in an instant. She could feel him very close behind her as she looked out at the water. She had the strangest urge to lean back against him, to feel herself supported by his warm, solid body.

As if reading her mind, he rested his hands on her shoulders and she felt herself beginning to relax. They stood there without speaking for what seemed to Olivia like quite a long time. Then she felt Jonas's cheek brushing tentatively against her hair as he bent his head to whisper quietly in her ear. "Last night, when we were finally alone together, everything went haywire. Let's just get to know each other a little better and see what happens from there. Marsha and Brad can take a slow boat to China for all I care, honest. I have absolutely no respect for a man who would pick her over you, anyway."

"We were young and foolish, I suppose."

"Now you're older, but wiser. And that's why you're going to at least spend the day with me."

She had to laugh at his persistence. If he went after accounts with this kind of single-minded determination, it was hardly any wonder that he drove around in a Mercedes. "No, Jonas, you've only got it partly right. I'm older, but obviously still *no* wiser. That's why I'm going to come with you."

His arms stole around her in a great bear hug as he tenderly pressed his lips to her cheek. "Well, let's hit the road, woman. I can't wait to help you smear on that sun-block lotion."

"I've never had any trouble managing on my own," she replied as he tossed some bills on the table to cover the check.

"Well, I always welcome a helping hand," he said as he ushered her back to the car. "To get at those hard-to-reach spots," he added with a mischievous gleam in his eye.

"Why don't you close your eyes and relax?" Jonas suggested once they were on the road. "The house is about an hour and a half from here."

Olivia was already having some difficulty keeping her eyes open and now she closed them all the way, reclining the car seat and laying her head back on the headrest. "Tell me something, Jonas," she murmured sleepily a few minutes later, "how in the world did you know I was checking out this morning?"

Jonas glanced over at her and laughed. "Last night, after I left your room, it seemed clear that you were capable of anything, including murdering me in my sleep."

Maybe not murder, Olivia replied silently, but something frightfully close to it.

"Foiling your great escape plan was a simple matter of persuading the desk clerk to cooperate with me, then making sure I was packed and ready to go once he sounded the alarm."

Olivia's eyes opened wide. "You mean that space cadet at the front desk was in cahoots with you the whole time?"

"That kid wasn't as dumb as he looked, believe me. He didn't come cheap."

Olivia stared at him for a moment, dumbstruck. "You're really unbelievable, Jonas," she said finally, as she settled back and closed her eyes again.

"I'll take that as a compliment."

"I didn't mean it that way," she countered.

"You will," he promised. They were the last words Olivia heard before she drifted off to sleep.

Four

And this is the master bedroom," Jonas said, leading the way into a spacious, airy room decorated in shades of soft gray and pastel blue. "The view from this deck is really great. Here, take a look." He pulled open the sliding glass door, allowing Olivia to walk out first.

The blue-green expanse of the Pacific stretched out before her as far as the eye could see. The house itself was built on a small cliff, and Olivia could see a flight of wooden steps that led from a lower deck down to the beach. She couldn't wait to stretch out under the hot sun, and she was suddenly glad that she had taken Jonas up on his invitation.

"That water looks wonderful. I can't wait to take a swim."

He smiled at her. "I'll bring up your bags right away then. As soon as you get settled and changed we can go down."

"Fine," Olivia replied as they went back into the bedroom.

"There's a sauna and whirlpool bath right through that door," he told her. "I'll show you how to work them later, if you like."

"All the comforts of home," Olivia said, her gaze falling upon the wide, white oak platform bed. Was he under the mistaken impression that she was going to share this room with him? "My, this is really lovely," she said, admiring an antique armoire.

Jonas came up beside her. "There's plenty of space inside." He swung open one of the doors. "If you want to hang some of your clothes in here."

"Oh, that would be rather silly, don't you think?"

"Silly?"

"I'm sure I'll be able to make do with whatever closet space you have in your guest room, Jonas. After all, it's only one night," she rambled on in the tone of the world's most accommodating houseguest. "I wouldn't dream of putting you out of your room," she said sweetly.

His chagrined expression confirmed Olivia's suspicions. "Yes...uh, the guest room," he said finally, "is that second door on the left." He gestured toward a doorway at the opposite end of the hall. "There's not much of a view from that side of the house," he warned her with a hopeful note in his voice. "Not nearly as nice as the other bedroom."

"It will be just fine, Jonas," she assured him. "After all, what can a person really see at night?" she asked innocently, as she turned to hide her smile.

"Right," he mumbled, heading for the stairs. "I'll go get the bags."

Olivia strolled down the hallway to the designated door. You couldn't blame a guy for trying, she thought as she fought to keep from laughing out loud.

A short time later, Olivia was stretched out on a beach towel she had found in her bathroom. She was wearing a sea-green maillot and about half a bottle of suntan lotion. The sun beat down fiercely and she could feel her body gratefully soaking up the warmth. As far as she knew, Jonas was still upstairs, pouting over her reluctance to take in the *view* from his bedroom. He would appear shortly, she had no doubt. One thing she liked about Jonas, he never wasted time sulking. He could always be counted on to bounce right back with some new plan of attack.

The thought had not quite left her mind when Olivia suddenly felt someone—or something—ardently licking her thigh. She sprang up from her prone position to come nose to nose with one of the largest, furriest, most wolflike dogs she had ever set eyes upon. While Olivia stared mesmerized at the size and number of its teeth, the beast leaned over, licked her forehead, then sat back on its haunches with a doggy-looking smile.

"That's two tastes...I hope you're not planning on taking a bite," Olivia said blithely. The dog shifted a bit on its front paws, continuing to stare at her with what she considered to be a very hungry look in its big brown eyes.

"Zeke! Stop bothering Olivia!"

Olivia turned to see Jonas, jogging up the shoreline toward her, wearing light blue running shorts and sunglasses. The dog instantly bounded toward him, kicking up sand in all directions. As Jonas approached, the dog ran in circles around him, racing through the surf with tireless energy.

Jonas walked up to Olivia's towel and sat down. "Sorry if he scared you," he apologized. "It must be your suntan lotion. He's usually not that friendly with strangers."

"My suntan lotion?"

Jonas nodded, then leaned over and lightly sniffed her shoulder. "You smell like a piña colada. Zeke just can't resist anything that's coconut-flavored. He's usually much better behaved than that."

The words had no sooner left his lips than Zeke trotted up beside them, looked adoringly at Jonas, then gave his body a good long shake, spraying water and wet sand all over both of them.

Ignoring their cries of protest, the dog proceeded to wedge himself between Jonas and Olivia, then lay down, taking up most of the towel, his long body hanging off either end. Panting, he looked up again at his master for approval.

"Did it take long to teach him that?" Olivia removed her sand-coated sunglasses and tried to clean them off with the corner of the towel. "I've never actually seen a dog trained to harass houseguests... but then again, this is California."

Jonas looked at Olivia and then back down at his dog. "Zeke, you are a bad dog," he announced in a somber, ominous tone. "A very bad dog."

Olivia felt unaccountably guilty for coming between man and his best friend. "You don't have to go on and on about it, Jonas. You're going to give the poor beast a complex."

Zeke, who had been resting his head on his paws during Jonas's scolding, now wriggled closer to Olivia and placed his head in her lap.

Olivia and Jonas looked at each other. "Look at him—the big lug. He always falls hard for redheads," Jonas said with a knowing sigh. "He's crazy about the Irish setter a few houses down the beach."

"Well, I hope it doesn't break his heart when he finds out I'm not registered with the American Kennel Club." She looked into Zeke's eyes and gave his head a pat.

"I'll try to break it to him very gently when we're alone together later," Jonas promised. He stood up and offered a hand to Olivia. "Come on, let's take a swim and get some of this sand off." Olivia allowed herself to be helped up, then walked down to the water hand in hand with Jonas.

"It's colder than I thought." Olivia was barely ankle deep and stopped in her tracks.

"Cold? It's beautiful, the perfect temperature." Jonas argued.

"You go ahead—I'll just ease my way in."

"Oh, you'll never get in like that. Let's run. I'll meet you on the other side of that wave."

Olivia, who preferred to swim in water that was no cooler than a tepid bath, thought Jonas must be part polar bear if he considered this the perfect temperature. "I think I'll—"

"It's not a matter of thinking, Olivia," Jonas said with stolid determination as he leaned over and swept her up into his arms. "That's where you make your mistake," he said, plodding steadily toward the crashing waves.

"What in the— Let me down! Are you crazy?" Olivia tried to get loose, but his hold was much too strong. "Are you trying to drown me or something?" she squealed.

"When your whole body is underneath you'll definitely feel warmer. Trust me."

Zeke, who'd followed them into the water, now hopped up and playfully nipped at Olivia's feet. "Jonas, I really don't want to—"

"Shut your mouth, Olivia dear. Here we go." Before Olivia could protest she felt herself immersed in the bone-chilling water. As a wave came crashing down near them, Jonas released her. Despite her denials, Olivia happened to be a very strong swimmer. She was especially adept at holding her breath. Spotting Jonas a short distance away after the wave had passed, she decided that she would teach him a lesson about dragging unwilling victims into the Pacific.

"Oh my goodness, I've got a cramp," she cried, flailing her arms a bit for emphasis.

Jonas, who had been swimming toward her, now doubled his efforts. "Hold on. I'll be right there. Don't panic," he called out to her.

Taking a deep breath Olivia slipped below the surface and swam underwater, passing Jonas. When she couldn't hold her breath for another instant, she popped up, finding herself quite a few yards from Jonas, who was by now frantically wondering where she had gone.

"I think I've worked that cramp out now," she announced, gracefully treading water.

Jonas spun around, the panic-stricken look on his face turning first to relief, then to pure menace. "Why you little—what are you trying to do, give me a heart attack?"

He paddled toward her with a dangerous look in his eye. Olivia stopped laughing and started swimming as fast as she could in the opposite direction. Jonas's broad shoulders and legs allowed him to cut through the water with ease. Somewhat winded from her underwater trickery, Olivia could see that he was rapidly gaining on her.

Soon they were side by side and Jonas remained undeterred by Olivia's fierce splashing. "So you had a little cramp," he said, his arm snaking out to pull her toward him. "Where exactly was it? Over here?" he asked, tickling her rib cage.

"Jonas, please don't..." With one arm pinned to her side Olivia had no choice but to hang on to Jonas with the other just to keep her head above water. "I hate to be tick—"

"Or maybe it was over here," he said, pinching her backside.

"Ouch!" She tried to slap at his shoulder with her free hand but only succeeded in splashing herself in the face.

She looked up into Jonas's laughing face and her irritation immediately dissolved into laughter as well. Their bodies were pressed intimately together beneath the water's surface as Jonas wrapped his other arm around her waist and Olivia clung to his broad shoulders.

Their laughter stopped as for a moment they stared into each other's eyes. Olivia had the strangest feeling of being suspended momentarily in time. With only the sparkling water and clear sky surrounding them, she felt as if she and Jonas had been transported to a world all their own.

"Don't ever scare me like that again."

She nodded, suddenly unable to speak. He leaned over and kissed her, tentatively at first, as if just sampling the salty taste on her lips. The moment his lips touched hers, Olivia had the startling realization that she'd been longing for his kiss all morning. Longing to reexperience the purely magical feelings he had ignited within her last night.

Their kiss grew deeper, their legs intertwining under the water in an intimate, arousing dance. "Olivia..." He sighed, finally pulling away. "If we keep this up we're both going to drown." Kissing the tip of her nose, he released her. "Let's go lie in the sun and I'll massage your cramp."

"I didn't have one and you know it," Olivia answered, laughing but reluctant to let him go.

"Well if I fix you a very nice lunch later, maybe you can pretend to have one again." Jonas smiled slyly as he set off in the direction of the beach. Seawater ran in rivulets down his face, glistening on his chest and arms.

Olivia tried to ignore the seductive sparkle in his eyes, but the heady effect of their kiss still lingered. Putting her head down in the water, she also set out for the beach, swimming almost parallel to Jonas, until they reached the breakers and it was everyone for himself. Olivia waited just before the point where the waves crashed, and watched for her chance to ride one in. She hadn't done this for years and wondered if she would get it right. Once the wave approached, her body seemed to remember exactly what to do. With her arms extended straight above her head, she felt herself propelled forward by the ocean's force, borne high on the very crest of the swell, then carried up to the shoreline through the swirling white foam. After the whole process was over, she remembered hearing somebody scream the way people do on roller-coaster rides and realized it was herself.

Jonas was there to meet her, helping her up from the soft sand before the powerful undertow carried her back into the sea. "You rode that wave in like a pro," he observed with genuine admiration in his tone. "Who would have suspected that I'm entertaining a bodysurfing champion?"

His praise was a bit lavish, considering her abilities, but she enjoyed it nonetheless. Her legs felt rubbery when she took a step, but the rest of her felt refreshed and thoroughly exhilarated. "We all have our hidden assets," she answered lightly as she lifted her arms to smooth back her wet hair.

Grinning, Jonas looked down to the top of her strapless suit.

"Not to mention those unhidden assets, champ," he teased. Olivia followed his gaze to find that the force of the water had pulled down her suit to just a breath away from indecent exposure. With a hasty motion she yanked it back up. Stifling a laugh, Jonas flung his arm around her shoulders and pulled her next to him as they walked back up toward the house.

While Jonas was inside getting more towels, Olivia took advantage of the enclosed, outdoor shower to clean off the saltwater, and the sand that had found its way into her suit. She then climbed the wooden stairs to the house's lower deck and made herself comfortable in a blue and white lounge chair. While the breeze and hot sun dried her off, she took a moment to admire Jonas's impressive home.

The wood and glass structure was boldly modern in design, yet lacked that cold, institutional look Olivia disliked about so many modern houses. Beyond the sliding glass doors that opened onto the deck, there was a large living room with a stone fireplace taking up one entire wall. The floors throughout the house were of terra-cotta tile, covered with brightly woven area rugs. Jonas had chosen the paintings and wall hangings from American Southwest artists and also had a few abstract pieces to complement the decor.

Olivia had also noticed many small personal touches in each room—a basket of seashells, a cluster of well tended plants—that told her Jonas was a man who cared about the place he lived in. He obviously preferred the homey, comfortable style he had achieved to the plastic, decorator look so many businessmen of her acquaintance opted for. This was definitely a point in his favor in her book.

"What are you so deep in thought about?" Jonas appeared at the doorway, with a stack of towels under one arm and carrying a tray of tall, cool-looking drinks. Olivia rose to help him and carried the tray to a round white table shaded by a huge white umbrella. "I was just admiring your house."

"Thank you. I helped design it," he said proudly. "I had a few drafting courses in college and worked some construction jobs then during the summers. I always dreamed about having a house like this, with the waves coming right up to my doorstep." He handed Olivia a drink and then sat down next to her.

"And here you are.... It's not everyone who can see their wishes come true."

"Except for one very important missing detail. One that no architect or decorator in the world could help me with."

Olivia was puzzled. "The place looks perfect to me," she said, taking a sip of her drink.

"Oh, it's got all the fancy hardware, from central air conditioning to a state-of-the-art food processor... I'm just missing the right person to share it with, that's all."

Olivia sighed mentally. The conversation was veering in a direction she preferred to avoid. Jonas's telling glance was beginning to stir up feelings and thoughts she didn't want to acknowledge. After all, what was the sense of starting something? They would only be together until tomorrow. Who knew when she might see him again, or even if his feelings were sincere. It all seemed too difficult, even though it wasn't hard at all to imagine him as a permanent part of her life.

"This drink is really delicious," she said, suddenly changing the subject and taking another sip. "What's in it?"

Jonas shrugged. "A lot of different fruits and juice. Some sherbet and crushed ice... and whatever else strikes my fancy at the moment. I'm not one for following a recipe when I cook. I just kind of go with the mood."

Olivia shook her head in dismay. "Maybe that's my trouble. I try to follow the recipe exactly... as if I was a chemist or something. Once I tried to make Thanksgiving dinner and the turkey exploded."

"Exploded?" Jonas asked, laughing. "What did you season it with, gunpowder?"

"I don't know what happened," Olivia said, as indignantly as if the event had occurred only yesterday. "I just opened the oven door and I was kind of poking at it. The next thing I knew—caboom. There was stuffing and giblets all over the apartment."

Jonas was chuckling so hard he had difficulty answering her. "What kind of stove was it, gas or electric?"

"I don't remember now. Would it make a difference?"

"Of course," he began to explain, amazed at her lack of knowledge. "With a gas stove—"

"Oh, don't even bother," Olivia cut in. "Believe me, I'm a lost cause in the kitchen."

"Don't worry, sweetheart. Where you're concerned, the kitchen is probably the *last* room I ever think about. Would you like another one of these?" he asked politely, raising his empty glass.

"I'm fine, thanks," she replied, still pondering the inference of his remark.

"Well, I'm ready for some serious tanning," he said, tossing Olivia two big towels and taking two for himself.

"Lead the way," Olivia replied agreeably. Following Jonas down the steps and across the hot sand, they laid out their towels side by side close to the water's edge. Olivia found her bottle of sun block tangled up in the towel Zeke had made a mess of earlier, and squeezed a generous pool of lotion in her hand. She methodically covered her legs, front and back, from her toes to the edges of her high-cut suit, then turned her attention to her arms, chest and neck. Propped up on one arm, Jonas watched, his attention riveted to the entire performance.

"I think you missed a spot," he offered genially. "The back of your left thigh, right above that adorable little birthmark. Want me to get it for you?"

"No, thank you." He really was impossible. Did he have to watch her do this as if she was on stage? "Enjoying yourself?"

He shrugged. "I just don't want you to get a bad sunburn, that's all. It's part of my duty as your host. Now, if you'll be a good guest and roll over," he said, taking the bottle of lotion from her hand, "I'll do your back."

Olivia, who knew that her back would be streaked with sunburned patches if she tried to do it herself, turned to lie down on her stomach. Resting her head on her arms, she closed her eyes. She felt Jonas's strong hands smoothing on the cool lotion, gently massaging her back from her neck down to the bottom of her spine. Letting him touch any part of her was a dangerous thing to do, she realized. It seemed to Olivia that any place Jonas made contact with suddenly became an erogenous zone.

Summoning her fading willpower, Olivia pushed herself up on her arms and sat facing him. "I think that will be just fine, thank you," she said, plucking the bottle from his hand.

"My pleasure, entirely. Now, if you would be so kind," he said, turning to lie down again, "I could use some of that on my back, too."

"Of course." She poured out some lotion into her hand and then began to dab it on his back in the most delicate, matter-of-fact fashion she could manage.

"You could rub a little harder," he suggested.

Olivia gave up trying to fake her way through the task, and finally allowed her hands to make full contact with Jonas's skin, smoothing the sun block over the sinewy contours of muscle. Very soon she let her guard down and actually began taking pleasure in running her hands over his well-developed physique.

Jonas, his cheek resting on his folded arms, sighed like a contented cat. "Mmm—that's more like it," he murmured encouragingly.

Olivia suddenly got hold of herself and sat back. "All done," she announced. "I guess you can handle the rest yourself. She dropped the bottle of lotion barely an inch from his nose and then stretched out on her back.

"I guess I'll have to," he grumbled. Olivia closed her eyes and tried to keep from smiling too widely. "Though I'd much prefer that you'd handle it," he muttered to himself.

"Did you say something, Jonas?" Olivia pretended she hadn't heard him.

"Nothing. Nothing at all," he replied in an overly sweet tone.

Olivia rested, allowing her thoughts to wander. Jonas hadn't said anything for a while so she opened her eyes and glanced over at him. He was sound asleep, turned on his side, facing her. She wondered if he'd originally been watching her while she rested. Somehow, it was strangely touching to think so—even though she couldn't understand exactly why she should feel that. Now she was the one watching Jonas sleep. His big, powerful body looked so vulnerable, his thick hair tousled from the wind, his heavy eyelashes curled against his cheeks like a child's.

He was a very unusual man, she thought, a unique mixture of boyish exuberance and a man's strength and will. When he wanted something—like this house for instance—she had the feeling that nothing could stand in his way. He wanted her, she knew that much. But whether it was for a night or for longer, and whether her connection to Brad Carmichael had anything to do with it, she honestly couldn't say. She felt her suspicions gradually melting and saw herself falling under the spell of Jonas's irrepressible warmth and charm. If she landed a role in a California-based show, a long-term relationship with Jonas wouldn't be so farfetched. Then she stopped herself from thinking any further in that direction. She hadn't even set foot in Los Angeles yet, for heaven's sake. Acting was a tough, competitive business, and Olivia knew from bitter experience that planning your life around maybes was only setting yourself up for disappointment.

She stared at Jonas again, suppressing an urge to reach out and smooth his hair back from his forehead. From where she sat, it didn't look as if their acquaintance could evolve into anything more than a very passionate one-night stand, which was not Olivia's style at all. Jonas had only been partly right when he said that if they didn't get to know each other better, they'd both regret it. She was getting to know him better and now had a whole new spectrum of regrets to contend with.

Before Olivia could work herself into a totally maudlin state of mind, Zeke trotted over to the edge of her towel and sat down, gently nudging her shoulder with a red Frisbee that was clasped between his jaws.

"All right, I'll give it a try." She stood up and took the Frisbee from his mouth. "But I think you should know I'm not very good at throwing one of these."

Undaunted by Olivia's disclaimer, Zeke galloped down to the shoreline, where she guessed he was used to playing catch with Jonas. Their game consisted of Olivia tossing the Frisbee, which sometimes landed close enough to Zeke that he could catch it in his mouth. Other times it flew at weird angles and landed in the shallow, white foam, where Zeke would eagerly dive in after it. After each toss, Olivia would be obliged to chase Zeke around for a few minutes to get the Frisbee back, which definitely seemed to be the dog's favorite part of the game.

"Okay, this is the last one," she said, panting as she flung the Frisbee toward him. It was a straight toss. Jumping up on his hind legs, Zeke caught it easily. As Olivia turned to walk back up the beach, the dog came bounding toward her. Eager to continue their game, he leaped up and put both paws on her shoulders. Olivia felt herself falling backward into the water, but at the last moment something stopped her. She felt herself encircled by Jonas's strong arms and recognized his touch before hearing his voice.

"Get down, you dumb mutt." He waved Zeke away with one hand. "Looks like I can't leave you two alone for a minute," he said to Olivia.

"He just wanted to play." Jonas had left his arm around her shoulder as they walked back up the shoreline. His embrace felt very comfortable and right.

"You've got to be firm with that dog, Olivia. When he wants something, he just won't take no for an answer."

"Just like his master," she observed. "You know, I've often heard that pets tend to absorb the personalities of their owners, but this is the first time I've ever seen such a startling example."

"With one important difference, my dear. Zeke is much better trained. When I want something, I won't be put off by a rap on the nose with a rolled-up newspaper."

Olivia glanced up to read the unspoken message in his eyes. She saw a look of hungry desire that disturbed her as much as it excited her. It was only afternoon, she realized, but as evening approached, she would be forced to confront both Jonas's feelings and her own.

Up at the house, Jonas fixed a salad for lunch while Olivia set the table outside. Their conversation was pleasant and light, though the ever-present tension of their attraction charged the atmosphere.

They'd gotten onto the subject of Jonas's work. At Olivia's bidding he had been regaling her with story after story of his escapades in the high-pressure sphere of advertising.

Although Olivia was certainly interested in what he had to say, she found herself continually distracted by Jonas's most mundane gestures, such as the way he held his knife and fork, the tiny lines that creased at the edges of his eyes when he smiled, the way he bowed his head and wrinkled his brow when he was trying to formulate a thought. She would not even have noticed these tiny details in some other man, but they suddenly seemed very special because they were Jonas's.

"...So I very sedately climbed out of the swimming pool, still in my tuxedo, with a sopping wet cigar in my mouth. And of course, Malcolm Phipps, who happened to be our biggest account at the time, was standing right there, waiting for some explanation of my behavior."

"What did you say?" Olivia asked, laughing.

"I said, 'Sir, if I'd had any idea at all that that woman was your daughter, this would have never happened.' And he said, 'Young man, you are mistaken, that woman is not my daughter...she's my *wife*. Please leave the premises immediately.' For a minute there I thought the old guy was going to challenge me to a duel at sunrise, but I suppose he realized that taking his business to another firm was revenge enough."

Olivia could easily imagine a younger, brasher version of Jonas getting himself into just such a predicament. "Did you get fired on Monday when you went into the office?" she asked him.

He shook his head. "At least I had the good sense to do the honorable thing, even back then. I phoned up my boss and resigned on Sunday morning." He smiled wistfully at the recollection of his youthful mistakes. "But I must be boring you to death with these stories."

"Not at all." Olivia thought she could listen to him talk all afternoon, though she was not quite ready to admit it. "What made you interested in advertising in the first place, Jonas? Is that what you studied in college?"

"No, I was a literature major in college with high hopes of a future as Professor Jonas Harper, Renaissance scholar. My senior year I even walked around campus in a tweed sport jacket, smoking a pipe."

"Honestly? No, you're fooling me again, Jonas. I can see it in your eyes."

"Don't believe me, huh?" With a thoughtful expression on his face he rubbed his jaw for a moment, then looked up at her once more. "Okay, how about this? 'Shall I compare thee to a summer's day? Thou art more lovely and more temperate.'" He continued to recite the sonnet flawlessly, down to the very last line, while Olivia sat in wide-eyed astonishment. Jonas was hardly the type of man she would have expected to know any poetry much less Shakespeare's love sonnets—by heart.

"Now if that's not proof enough for you, let me just add that the letter *e* appears fifty-three times in that poem. Since I did a sixty-page term paper on this sonnet—and no one *but* an aspiring scholar would dream of wasting his time on such an effort—I consider that sufficient proof for anyone."

"I'm convinced," Olivia replied fervently. "But I still don't see the connection between Shakespeare and—"

"Composing the jingle for Tender Touch toilet tissue?" he cut in. "Yes, I can see where that might be confusing. Well, to make a long story short, for various reasons I became disillusioned with the vision of Professor Harper, Shakespearean scholar. But I never lost my love for poetry, for musical compositions out of words. I even still write some poetry myself," he confessed.

Reciting Shakespeare was one thing, but Olivia was astonished by this latest admission. Once she thought about it, however, it made sense. Ever since she had met Jonas, she had glimpsed a sensitive, romantic spirit beneath his glib, smooth-talking personality. Now she was beginning to see a whole new side of him, a side that she liked very much.

"Would you recite one of your poems for me, Jonas?" she asked quietly.

"Now?" She nodded. He looked into her eyes to see if she was serious, then looked away. "Well, I—no, I'm sorry. I really couldn't," he finally replied, looking down at his dish. Olivia couldn't tell for sure, but it seemed to her that he was actually blushing. Somehow the sight of Jonas's shy reaction was very touching. For once, he was at a loss for a clever comeback.

"Maybe some other time then," she said lightly.

"Sure." He smiled at her, his outgoing, exuberant self once more. "It must be hard to do what you do, getting up in front of a lot of people and acting, I mean. Aren't you frightened?"

Olivia smiled. "It's a little scary," she admitted. "But only just before I get on stage. Once I'm out there it's as if I'm another person entirely. I have to concentrate so hard on being that other person that there's really no room left in my mind to be scared. It's hard to explain exactly," she said, searching for the right words. "It's almost as if a switch clicks inside me."

Jonas nodded thoughtfully. "I think I understand what you mean. But it still takes guts, if you ask me."

"Not guts exactly... most actors are very shy people, in fact. You should have seen me in high school." She rolled her eyes skyward. "I think I was voted girl most likely to blend in with the wallpaper."

"Come on, Olivia. I can't believe that. I'll bet you were one of those snooty prom queens, who were swamped with dates."

"Prom queen?" Olivia laughed. "More like nerd queen, Tuckahoe High, Class of '72."

"Well, as my aunts and uncles used to say, 'you've filled out very nicely, dear,'" he replied with an admiring glance. "What happened in between? Did your fairy godmother finally put in an appearance?"

"During my freshman year in college she tapped me with a magic wand full of hormones. As my dear old granny often promised me, I was just a late bloomer after all."

"Granny sounds like a very smart cookie."

"She's a dear. She brought us up—my brother Todd and me. My mother died when I was about five and my dad never really got over it. He traveled a lot on business, all over the world, for months at a stretch. We didn't see him much, even though he always brought us home fabulous presents."

"That must have been pretty rough," Jonas said sympathetically.

"I think it was harder for Todd, being a boy without a father. But my grandmother did her best—went to watch his baseball games and all that sort of thing. I've come to think that she gave us a better upbringing than most people have had in conventional families."

"She sounds pretty special. I'd like to meet her sometime. Does she still live in Tuckahoe?"

Olivia was taken aback a bit by Jonas's request. Sometimes he acted as if they really did have a future together—or more likely, she thought, he was just making pleasant conversation. "Yes, she still lives there. The same house I grew up in. She shares it now with one of her sisters, my Aunt Kate. Aunt Kate's very prim and fussy. They're kind of an octogenarian version of the odd couple."

Jonas laughed. "I suppose you became interested in acting after the great blossoming occurred."

"Oh, I was hooked on acting long before that, in high school, in fact. While most of my girlfriends were at the local drive-in, defending their virtue, I was reading scenes from Tennessee Williams and Noel Coward in the front parlor with Todd. It was fun to be someone different for a few hours—someone glamorous and exciting."

"Don't tell me," Jonas cut in. "Under Granny's direction, no doubt."

Olivia nodded and bit into one of the plump, ripe strawberries that Jonas had served for dessert in a carved-out pineapple half. "Granny had been on the stage in her youth in a traveling repertory group. That's how she met my grandfather."

"Was he an actor also?"

"No, but he loved the theater and thought nothing of traveling hours to see a play. He went all the way to Saratoga to see my grandmother's troupe perform *Othello*. After the last scene, when my grandmother— playing Desdemona—was strangled, he rushed backstage to make sure she was really all right. Or so he *said*," Olivia added with a sly smile. "He was a doctor."

"Who had a practice in Tuckahoe?" Jonas guessed.

Olivia nodded. "You got it. Gran always claimed it was love at first sight."

Jonas looked at her thoughtfully. "You sound as if you don't believe it's possible—love at first sight, I mean."

Olivia looked at him quizzically, suddenly alerted by the change in his tone. "Well—maybe for my grandparents it was..." she said, turning away from his steady gaze.

"But not for you?" he persisted.

"It hasn't happened yet," she replied lightly.

He continued to look at her, his fingers toying with the knife that rested against his plate. "Sometimes a person doesn't realize these things until after the fact," he informed her. "But at least that leaves out Brad Carmichael."

"Leaves him out of what?"

"You obviously didn't fall in love with him at first sight."

"I don't know if I was ever really in love with Brad," she answered quietly. "It all seems so long ago. Sometimes when I try to remember, it's like looking back through a fog."

"You were engaged to marry him, weren't you?" Jonas reminded her. "Last night was a bit confusing, but I think I got that much straight."

"Yes, we were engaged. I even had a ring, which I really didn't like to wear because I was always afraid I'd lose it. It was a minuscule diamond, actually," she said with a little laugh. "You almost needed a magnifying glass to see it."

"But it's the thought that counts," Jonas said dryly.

"Brad thought we would need our savings for more important practical things, once we were married," Olivia explained. "He always was very...uh..." She searched for the right word.

"Tightfisted? Frugal? Cheap?"

"Mature was the word I was looking for," Olivia cut in with a slight sharpness to her tone.

"And your family approved of him, of course."

"Everyone but Granny. She just never took to him. She thought he was a little too mature, if you know what I mean. She said she didn't want to see me get my wings clipped by a man with such 'bourgeois aspirations.'"

"Bravo, Granny. I'll thank her in person when we finally meet."

Olivia could easily see Jonas and her grandmother getting along famously. The vision was a bit too vivid for her peace of mind and she tried her best to ignore it. "Gran tended to get a bit dramatic at times. I think when Brad finally dumped me for Marsha she was quite pleased with the way things turned out. Oh, she was sorry for me, of course. Gave me a lot of petting and sympathy when I went home that summer. But she told me I'd get over it all in time . . . and I did," Olivia concluded brightly. "Except for having a slight relapse when I met Marsha yesterday." She shook her head. "I don't know why I just wasn't honest with her."

Jonas smiled and then reached over to pat her hand. "Nobody's perfect, sweetheart. Sometimes we think we've put the past behind us and we really haven't. It tends to spring up at us like a jack-in-the-box at the darnedest moments. Especially when our pride is concerned."

"Yes, I suppose you're right." Olivia smiled at Jonas, glad that he was so understanding about the

SILHOUETTE GIVES YOU SIX REASONS TO CELEBRATE!

MAIL THE BALLOON TODAY!

INCLUDING:

1.
4 FREE BOOKS

2.
AN ELEGANT MANICURE SET

3.
A SURPRISE BONUS

AND MORE!

TAKE A LOOK . . .

Yes, become a Silhouette subscriber and the celebratic goes on forever.

To begin with, we'll send you

- 4 new Silhouette Desire novels—FREE
- an elegant, purse-size manicure set—FREE
- and an exciting mystery bonus—FREE

And that's not all! Special extras— three more reasons to celebrate.

4. Money-Saving Home Delivery. That's right! When you subscribe to Silhouette Desire, the excitement, romance and faraway adventures of these novels can be yours for previewing in the convenience of your own home. Here's how it works. Every month, we'll deliver six new books right to your door. If you decide to keep them, they'll be yours for only $1.95 each. That's 30¢ less per book than what you pay in stores. And there's **no charge for shipping and handling.**

5. Free Monthly Newsletter. It's the indispensable insider's look at our most popular writers and their up-coming novels. Now you can have a behind-the-scenes look at the fascinating world of Silhouette! It's an added bonus you'll look forward to every month!

6. More Surprise Gifts. Because our home subscribers are our most valued readers, we'll be sending you additional free gifts from time to time—as a token of our appreciation.

This beautiful manicure set will be a useful and elegant item to carry in your handbag. Its rich burgundy case is a perfect expression of your style and good taste. And it's yours free in this amazing Silhouette celebration!

SILHOUETTE DESIRE®

FREE OFFER CARD

4 FREE BOOKS

ELEGANT MANICURE SET —FREE

FREE MYSTERY BONUS

PLACE YOUR BALLOON STICKER HERE!

MONEY-SAVING HOME DELIVERY

FREE FACT-FILLED NEWSLETTER

MORE SURPRISE GIFTS THROUGHOUT THE YEAR—FREE

Yes! Please send me my four Silhouette Desire novels **FREE**, along with my manicure set and my **free mystery gift**. Then send me six new Silhouette Desire novels every month and bill me just $1.95 per book (30¢ less than retail), with no extra charges for shipping and handling. If I am not completely satisfied, I may return a shipment and cancel at any time. **The free books, manicure set and mystery gift remain mine to keep.**

CBD017

NAME
(PLEASE PRINT)

ADDRESS   APT.

CITY   STATE

ZIP

Terms and prices subject to change.
Your enrollment is subject to acceptance
by Silhouette Books.

SILHOUETTE "NO RISK GUARANTEE"
• There is no obligation to buy—the free books and gifts remain yours to keep.
• You pay the lowest price possible—and you receive books before they're available in stores.
• You may end your subscription anytime—just let us know.

crazy charade she had gotten him involved in. She realized another man might not have been so good about it. Another man might not have been so easy to talk with for the past few hours about any number of very private and sensitive topics. She felt so relaxed around Jonas, so much herself, it was as if they had known each other for years.

"Besides, if you had been honest with Marsha yesterday, we would have never met. So I have two reasons to thank her, come to think of it."

"Two? What's the first?"

"Stealing Brad Carmichael away from you," he explained with a crooked smile. "You're not the type of woman who should have her wings clipped by any man."

"I'm very careful about my wings these days. But thanks for your concern." They were both silent for a moment, then Olivia said, "Speaking of Brad and Marsha—what are your plans now concerning the Multi-Foods account?"

Jonas shrugged. "I told you this morning, Olivia, I have no plans at all regarding Carmichael's advertising. I suppose I'll have to call the hotel in San Diego tomorrow and make some explanation for backing out of my invitation."

"Yes, you did promise to call with directions, didn't you?" Olivia found it difficult to believe that Jonas—who had been literally frothing at the mouth over the possibility of winning this account last night—could so easily turn his back on it now. His mind seemed firmly set about it, though. "You could still go see him in San Francisco, of course. I remember him asking you to come up in a week or two."

"Yes, he did say that. But I'm not planning on making the trip. There'll be other Brad Carmichaels to go after, believe me. I'm not worried in the least about letting this one go," he assured her.

Though his words seemed sincere enough, Olivia somehow had the feeling that there was more behind Jonas's decision than he was willing to confide.

"Is it because you're suddenly lacking a wife? I suppose that makes the whole thing more complicated."

"No, that's not it at all. I could easily manage without you—at least long enough to get the contract." He suddenly released her hand and pushed his seat back from the table. It made a sharp scraping sound on the deck that seemed appropriate to the sudden feeling of tension that had developed between them. "My reasons are much more complicated than that, Olivia. I'm not at all sure that I want to explain them to you."

He stood up and began piling the dirty dishes onto a tray. Olivia rose also and tried to do what she could to help him. While Jonas loaded the dishwasher and straightened out the kitchen, Olivia carried in the remaining dishes and leftovers from outside.

Their conversation was reduced to the bare minimum necessary to complete the work at hand. Olivia couldn't say that Jonas seemed exactly angry, he was just distracted and distant. Very unlike the warm, personable man who had been going all out to entertain her for most of the day. She felt strangely robbed of that warmth, but at a loss to understand how to get Jonas back to his old self again.

It was the last part of their conversation that had disturbed him. She wondered if, in his mind, Jonas had made some choice between her and the biggest chunk of business he had ever stumbled across in his life. Last night she certainly wouldn't have believed him capable of such noble sentiments. But now she had come to see a whole new side of him. A side she would never have expected. As a professional, she was especially aware when a man was putting on an act to make himself more appealing. But that was not the case with Jonas. The more she discovered about him, the more time she spent in his company, the more dangerously appealing she found him.

Five

"What are you doing with that?" Olivia eyed the huge pot that Jonas had just pulled out of the closet. It looked suspiciously like a witch's caldron and she wondered what was on the menu.

"I'm going to fill it with water, like this," Jonas said, setting it in the sink and turning on the faucet. "Then, I'm going to put it on the stove, and when the water is hot enough, we're both going to jump in. Since you refused to get in the hot tub upstairs with me, I thought this contraption might be more in tune with your kinky, nonorganic, New York tastes." He punctuated his brief speech by slamming down the pot's sizable metal cover.

"Just curious," Olivia answered calmly. She watched Jonas stalk about the kitchen. She couldn't believe he was still in a bad mood over their most recent tiff. They had gone for a late-afternoon swim and had done some more relaxing on the beach after lunch.

When they returned to the house Olivia had excused herself to shower. Jonas had suggested that she join him in the whirlpool bath, which he had promised was an experience not to be missed. But Olivia—sorely tempted to join him—had diplomatically declined the invitation. Now she could see that her rejection, which Jonas had gracefully accepted, had stung a bit more than he had let on.

Let him think I'm the world's biggest prude, if that's what he wants to believe, she thought. In her heart she knew that it wasn't Jonas she had been afraid of. Mostly, it was herself.

To make matters even worse, Jonas's surly mood seemed to make him look even more attractive. His damp hair was combed back from his forehead and made his strong features look almost like those of a classical Greek sculpture. He'd changed into white shorts and a loose-fitting, cream-colored cotton shirt. It conjured up images of pirates, Olivia thought, which wasn't all that out of synch with the scowl on his face.

Jonas glanced over at her, then bent his head inside the refrigerator. "You don't have to stay in here and watch me. Considering your profound dislike of cooking, I would think that this is the last place you'd want to be."

Olivia took a step forward. "I want to help. Maybe pick up a few tips." He glanced over at her with a look of disbelief. "Honest," she added.

For a moment she didn't think he had heard. Then he emerged from the depths of the refrigerator, his arms loaded with vegetables, which he carried over to the counter near the sink.

"All right, if you really want to." He reached into a drawer and removed two folded aprons, handing one over to Olivia. "You don't want to get that dress dirty. It's very pretty," he added tersely.

"Thank you," Olivia said graciously. It was a pale pink, cotton-knit sundress with a skirt that reached nearly to her ankles. Deceptively simple in design, it clung lovingly to her every inch, doing wonderful things for her figure, her coloring and her self-esteem. The dress was a foolproof man-pleaser, and Olivia had no doubt that it would please the man she was dining with tonight. That was until Jonas had greeted her so coolly when she came downstairs. So he had noticed the dress, after all. Well, it's about time you got around to mentioning it, Bozo, she had the urge to reply. "It's just perfect for the weather out here," she said instead.

Jonas let his gaze skim over her quickly, from her freshly shampooed hair to her toes. He cleared his throat. "Yes, I can see that," he replied blandly, turning around to put on his apron.

Olivia smiled slightly, secretly pleased with herself. She unfolded the apron and put it on. "So? Where do we start?"

"Well, the first item on the menu is baked clams." Jonas reached into a paper bag and removed a large clam, holding it up between his forefinger and thumb for her inspection. "Here is Mother Nature's idea of the perfect airtight container. If you'll notice," he said, turning the clam from side to side, "there is no pop-top or twist-off lid on this little sucker."

"I've always thought Velcro would be the ideal solution myself," she commented solemnly, staring down at the clam.

"Maybe you can write somebody about that. In the meantime, we must make use of this." He reached into a drawer and removed a stubby, knife with a rounded-off blade. "A clam knife, used for prying open the little devils—otherwise known as clam shucking."

"Go on, I'm fascinated."

"It's very simple. You slip the blade in like so, then kind of wiggle it through," he demonstrated, "and *voilà*." Jonas valiantly wrestled with the clam, but nothing happened. "The clam, a highly underrated but very noble animal, will fight to defend his honor, of course."

"Of course," Olivia echoed solemnly. Laughter at this point would certainly insult Jonas, but it was very difficult for her to resist. "Why don't we tempt it open with some bait?" she suggested. "A cup of chowder maybe..."

Jonas made a face at her, intent as ever on the stubborn specimen. "There," he said proudly. "I've got it now." Finally, the clam had surrendered and lay open in his hand. "Now this is going to be your job,

so pay attention." Olivia looked up at him alertly.
"See that sand in there?" She looked at the place inside the gooey clam innards where he pointed and
nodded. "All you have to do is wash that out like
this." He turned on the tap and showed her how to do
it. "Then put the clam meat in this bowl and the shell
in that one. Got it?"

Olivia nodded, gulping back a hysterical reply that
would have sounded something like, You honestly
expect me to touch that slimy thing with my bare
hands? This was one of those parts of cooking that she
hated, but playing the role of an all-around good
sport, she gritted her teeth and got started. It could
have been much worse. Escargots or even squid, she
thought. She had only a few hours left in Jonas's
company and didn't want to spoil it. He certainly
looked as if he was in his glory, shucking away at his
pile of clams with ease. Besides, she had offered to
help him.

Just as the thought was passing through her mind,
Jonas turned to see how she was holding up. There was
something printed on his apron, she noticed. It read:
Rule No. 1: Never Volunteer. Then she looked down
at her own to see that it said: Rule No. 2: See Rule
No. 1.

"You can't say I didn't try to warn you."

"I'm a great one for reading signs after it's too
late," she replied glumly as Jonas handed her another clam to clean. "Oh, well, maybe I'll find a pearl
in one of these."

"Clams don't have pearls—those are oysters you're thinking of," he said, laughing.

"Well, there must be some employee benefits around here," she groused.

He smiled at her, a mischievous sparkle in his eye. "Don't worry, sweetheart. We'll get to that part in due time," he promised, handing over yet another mushy mollusk.

Olivia attended to her task, pretending not have heard him.

They continued with the dinner preparations, Jonas patiently explaining the steps of each recipe to his attentive pupil. Although Olivia knew she wasn't about to turn into Julia Child overnight, somehow it was much more fun to fool around in the kitchen with Jonas than it had ever been trying to interpret the baffling cookbook terminology on her own. Within about two hours they had prepared a meal of baked clams, steamed asparagus, wild rice and, for the entrée, Jonas surprised her by producing two very lively, wriggling lobsters.

"Oh my God!" She jumped back about three feet as he began to walk toward her, brandishing the lobsters, one in each hand.

"They're beauties, aren't they?" He held one out and she bit back a scream.

"Get away from me with that thing! Doesn't it have a leash or something?"

"Olivia, calm down." He filled the sink with water and tossed the lobsters in. "You have to cook lobsters when they're alive. Didn't you know that?"

"No, I didn't know that—you just had to show me how to work a vegetable peeler, remember?" She hesitantly stepped over to the sink and peered down at the captives. "They look very sad, Jonas. Honestly, I think they know what's going to happen."

He looked at the lobsters and then back at Olivia. "How in the world can a lobster look sad?" he finally asked. He shook his head as if to clear his mind of her infectious zaniness, then placed his hands firmly on her shoulders. "You just sit right over there and let me handle this alone. Have another glass of champagne while you're at it," he added, directing her toward a chair at the long, oak kitchen table.

In between their chopping and dicing, Jonas had opened a bottle of champagne—"for inspiration," he had explained—and had poured them each a glass. Olivia now lifted the delicate, tulip-shaped crystal glass as Jonas filled it once more. She sipped her wine and tried her best to keep from bothering Jonas.

"What are you going to do now?" she asked after a few moments.

"I'm just about ready to drop them in that pot of boiling water."

Oh, the caldron, she thought. What a fate. "Jonas?" she asked quietly, "do lobsters make any kind of sound when they get ... uh ..."

Jonas, who had been checking the rice, turned toward her, a wooden cooking spoon in one hand. "I allow them each one phone call, which they've already had while you were showering," he said very seriously. "If the governor doesn't call with a reprieve in about three minutes," he added, looking down at his watch, "in they go."

"I'm sorry. I'm being pretty silly, aren't I?" she said, looking down at her glass. "I mean, after you've gone to so much trouble to fix us such a lovely meal—"

"You mean *we* have fixed such a lovely meal," he cut in. When she looked up, he was smiling at her. "I can't remember when I've had this much fun cooking." With his glass in hand he came over and sat down next to her at the table.

"Really? I thought I was probably cramping your style—especially when I spilled those peppercorns all over the floor."

He took her chin in his hand and turned her face toward him so that she had no choice but to look directly in his sparkling hazel eyes. "I'll admit that I was extremely distracted while you bent over to clean them up, but cramp my style?" He shook his head slowly. "You're just my style, Olivia—in every way..."

Jonas leaned toward her and Olivia closed her eyes, savoring the warm pressure of his lips on her own. Turning toward him, she lifted her arm and ran her fingers through his thick, glossy hair. Their kiss deepened, tasting of champagne but affecting her instantly from head to toe in a far more devastating way than alcohol ever had.

"Hmmm, Olivia." Jonas sighed into her hair, trying to get as close as their awkward seating arrangement would allow. "I just want to hold you close and..."

Olivia, nearly mesmerized by Jonas's husky voice, opened her eyes slightly, still caught in a sensual haze of their shared emotions. Suddenly, she pulled back, her eyes wide with alarm, and pointed at the counter just behind him.

"Jonas, the lobsters! They got loose!"

Jonas spun around in his seat to see that the main course was definitely trying to make a run for it. While he tried to corner the crustacean that was crawling quickly across the long countertop, the other lobster fell into the open dishwasher and then onto the floor and then crept rapidly in Olivia's direction.

Jonas couldn't quite tell if Olivia was running toward the lobster or away from it. "Be careful now. I cut the rubber bands off their claws and they're not that easy to pick—ouch!" He jumped back, trying to shake the pain out of the finger the lobster had briefly caught hold of.

"Jonas, are you okay?" Olivia began to approach him, but he waved her away.

"I'm fine, really," he assured her. "You'd better watch that one. He's heading for the sun deck and the door is open."

Olivia grabbed a big basket that was hanging from a beam on the kitchen ceiling and charged after the swiftly departing entrée. Luring the lobster's claws away from his hands with a dish towel, Jonas finally got hold of his escapee and quickly tossed it into the pot of boiling water.

"Nice try, fella. But you never would have made it to the border alive," he said into the pot as he slammed on the cover.

"Jonas, help...quick! This thing has gotten hold of my dress!"

Jonas turned to see Olivia with her back pressed against the sliding glass door, holding the large basket in front of her like a gladiator's shield. The lobster had clamped one claw onto the hem of her long dress and was pulling with all of its crustacean might.

Nearly paralyzed with laughter at the sight, Jonas could do little more than stand by the sink and stare. "Hurry, will you please!" Olivia urged him.

A short time later they were seated across from each other out on the deck, enjoying their dinner by candlelight. Olivia found every bite uniformly delicious, and it was hard for her to believe that she'd actually helped make it. When Jonas finally brought out the cooked lobsters, neither of them said a word about the frantic roundup scene. But when he smiled at her as he served it, she had a feeling that he was also recalling their absurd kitchen adventure.

"How is everything?" he finally asked her.

"Delicious—my compliments to the chef."

"And the chef's apprentice," Jonas added with a smile. "I think we should drink a toast to them both." He lifted his glass as Olivia did the same, crystal meeting crystal with a pleasant-sounding ring. Jonas looked deeply into her eyes for a moment, his strong features softened by the candle's flickering light. Olivia felt the power of their attraction, a physical sensation welling up within her like the waves she could hear crashing on the beach below.

She looked back down at her dinner and ignored the very valid worries she had about the future whenever she considered her feelings for Jonas. Their conversation throughout the rest of the meal was light and relaxed. Olivia found this a refreshing change from her usual dinner chatter while on a date. When she socialized with fellow actors they were usually so vain and self-involved, they hardly noticed what was on the table. Or else they were so artistically intense and "sensitive" she was nearly bored to death. The young, up-and-coming business types were altogether different. But with them she usually felt as if she was being quizzed to see just how knowledgeable she was on the latest films, books, plays, fashionable restaurants and health clubs. Though certainly stimulating, an hour or so of that kind of banter left Olivia virtually exhausted.

But even when she talked about personal or serious topics with Jonas, she never felt as if they were straining to impress each other. Everything felt natural and honest, and Olivia knew that was rare and special. The more she thought about Jonas, the more difficult it became to visualize simply turning her back on him when she left the next day for Los Angeles.

After coffee and dessert, they cleaned up the kitchen and Jonas suggested a walk on the beach. Olivia welcomed the idea. She didn't know exactly how she was going to word her polite excuses and then make a dash for her room. Most of all, being perfectly honest with herself, she wasn't really ready to leave Jonas for the evening.

They walked along the shore hand in hand for quite some time before Jonas finally spoke. "So, are your plans still the same? I mean, do you still intend going up to Los Angeles tomorrow?"

Olivia didn't know what to say. Up until now, she had not allowed herself to consider staying with Jonas for another day, or even longer, though she was sure that he would ask her to. In spite of her feelings for him, she had thought that she would be able to answer him with a very quick, firm refusal when the moment finally arrived. Now here she was, torn between what she wanted to do and what she knew would be better for both of them in the long run.

"Yes," she quietly replied. "Even though I don't have any appointments until next week, there are a number of people I have to see while I'm there."

"Right." Olivia looked up to gauge his reaction, but Jonas's eyes looked straight ahead and it was difficult for her to tell what he was thinking. "You're in California on business after all, aren't you?"

"It's been terribly easy to forget so far, I must admit. But I did come out here to find another job."

"Yes, you did, didn't you? Why was that again? The character in your play is getting murdered, or something?"

"Not murdered. Charlotte Mae has a car accident while she's driving to take her blackmailer another suitcase full of loot. What happens is, after she dies, everyone finds out that she was really Judge Wilcox's illegitimate daughter, and her awful secret is revealed."

"Which is?"

Olivia shrugged. "I don't know. The writers haven't decided yet.... Besides, what does it matter? I mean, Charlotte Mae will be gone from our TV screens forever, and hopefully I'll be so busy with a new role I won't have time to worry about it." She sighed. "I've been playing Charlotte Mae for the past three years, so I suppose I'll shed a few tears when she bites the dust. But you really have to learn not to get too involved."

"That's show biz, I guess," Jonas added thoughtfully. "You're welcome to stay here another day or so, if you like. In fact, I'd like you stay very much."

The sincere and slightly hopeful tone in his voice was almost more than Olivia could stand. But she rallied her defenses and forced herself to close her mind to visions of the pleasures that a few more days in this man's company would bring. "I'd like to, Jonas. Honestly." She stopped walking and looked up at him. He seemed unable to meet her gaze, which made her feel even worse.

"Sure, I understand. Business is business, I guess."

"I had a great time today," she assured him. "A wonderful time. I want to thank you."

He shrugged. "No thanks necessary. It was my pleasure having you here... and Zeke's," he added with a slight smile, glancing at the dog who ran ahead of them along the shore. "Maybe you can stop and visit us next week, before you go back to New York."

"No, I don't think so," she replied, looking down at the sand. "I don't think I'll have the time," she lied.

"Just a thought," he said, putting his hands in his pockets. His voice was a bit cooler and more detached than before and Olivia felt horrible about hurting his feelings.

With a shrill whistle, Jonas called Zeke and they turned and began walking back toward the house. Jonas didn't reach for her hand as he had before, and Olivia felt even sadder. She was wearing a brightly colored woven shawl and now she wrapped it around her shoulders, feeling suddenly chilled. After such a lovely day, why did her time with Jonas have to end on such a sour note? It just didn't seem right.

"What do you look so worried about?" he asked as they approached the house. "Finding a new job?"

She shook her head. "I'm just sorry that I have to go," she confessed.

He sighed. "But not sorry enough to stay longer."

"Oh, Jonas, don't be like that. You know why I can't stay."

"No, I don't know." He stopped walking. Reaching out to lay one hand on her shoulder, he turned her around to face him. "Why don't you explain it to me?"

In the darkness it was hard to read his expression. She wondered if he was really angry, or only hurt and disappointed. A little of each, she decided. Besides, he wasn't the only one who found this situation disappointing. "I've already told you I have to be in L.A. to find a job."

"Don't give me that," he said angrily. "You know that's not the real reason."

"Oh really?" She could feel her temper rising. Why couldn't he just make this easy on both of them? "Why don't you tell me what it is then, if you're such a mastermind?"

"All right," he said, moving toward her through the dark. "It's just this." Wrapping his arms around her, he pulled her so close against his hard body that Olivia could feel every muscular inch of him pressed against her from head to toe. His mouth came down on hers in a bold, possessive kiss, one that seemed to urge her toward some unspoken admission that she desired him as much as he desired her. Olivia tried to hold herself back from responding, but she was finally unable to resist the seductive pressure of his lips on her own and the powerful effect of his nearness. Almost against her will, she felt her arms curving up around his back, drawing him even closer. He kissed her again and again, his hands moving up and down her body in a sensual, hypnotizing pattern of caresses. Olivia clung to him, feeling herself grow dizzy with longing. She was unable to pull away, or even to think about anything but the sweet, fiery sensation of Jonas's lips against her own. When he pulled her down to the sand beside him, she did not resist. Their bodies were parted only for an instant, yet somehow it felt like hours before she was again drawn against his warmth. On the cool, packed sand, Jonas cradled her against his chest with one arm while the other hand slipped beneath her shawl to trace the soft curves of her breast, waist and hips with a smooth, loving touch.

"This is why you're leaving, Olivia. Admit it," he whispered huskily. "You're afraid of what happens every time we touch, so you're running away."

"I am afraid," she admitted quietly. "There's no future to this. Can't you see that?"

"Is that what you're so worried about?" He stroked back her hair with his hand. "What if you get a good part, then you'll be living out here. Isn't that one possibility for the future?"

"And another is that I don't get a part and I go back to New York next week. Or haven't you considered that?"

"Don't you think I've thought of that?" he said almost angrily. "The future can be what we *want* it to be. Don't worry about it," he urged her. "Just think about us—how wonderful it feels when we're together like this." He blazed a path of delicate kisses from her temple down the soft curve of her jaw. "This doesn't happen to two people every day, sweetheart. Not to me, anyway...."

Or to me, Olivia wanted to say. But ironically, it was the strength of her desire for Jonas that kept her from surrendering to him totally. No matter what he believed, she saw nothing for them beyond one glorious, passion-filled weekend. If she thought it would be hard to leave Jonas tomorrow, how much more difficult would it be after having made love with him?

"No—I can't stay," she said finally. Pushing him away, she rose quickly and ran down the beach toward the house. Jonas called to her, but she didn't turn around. She could tell from the sound of his voice that he wasn't racing after her. When she reached the steps, she climbed up quickly to the deck, let herself in and went straight to her room.

Without turning the lights on, she dropped her shawl on a chair and stretched out facedown on the bed. She felt emotionally as well as physically drained. She was trying to block out the sound of Jonas's voice calling after her, which still echoed in her mind. She believed she had done the right thing. Yet that assurance was little comfort for a body that ached with unsatisfied longing.

A few minutes later, she heard a soft knock on the door. Her body tensed with alarm and she barely drew a breath. Jonas quietly said her name. He waited a moment, then called again. She didn't answer, yet he didn't walk away. She could almost feel his presence through the closed door and fought to resist a powerful urge to respond. Finally, she heard his footsteps as he walked down the hallway to his room.

Olivia reached up and turned on the lamp beside the bed. She felt windblown, gritty and, most of all, heartsick. She pulled off her clothes and dragged herself into the adjoining bathroom. Later, lying on the bed with the lights out, Olivia remained wide awake. She had a script in her valise that she needed to study for an audition, and she turned on the light again to find it. She didn't really feel like studying a role, but anything was preferable to lying awake in the dark, thinking about Jonas only a few yards down the hallway.

The script was for a new TV sitcom about two women who ran a bed and breakfast. Although the writing was definitely above average and Olivia did feel an affinity for the role she would possibly read for, she simply could not concentrate on the material for more than a line or two. When she found herself reading the same stage direction over for the fifth time, she finally tossed the script aside with a grunt of frustration and disgust.

She sat up in bed, hugging her knees. She felt restless and keyed up. It was ridiculous to try to sleep, she decided. The way she felt at that moment, she wondered if she would ever sleep again. She knew it was her own fault. As Jonas had once pointed out with such irritating accuracy, she was the one who had started this whole thing. With a roomful of men to choose from, she had picked him. For what reason—disregarding the fact that he was one of the sexiest, most attractive, absolutely magnetic men she had ever met, she amended—who could say? Well, as Gran always said, you made your bed and now you have to lie in it. But no one had ever warned her that she'd have to lie in it alone.

Bouncing up, Olivia pulled off her nightgown and pulled on a pair of jeans and a sweatshirt. She would be darned if she would sit up in this room all night, feeling stir crazy and mulling over her feelings for Jonas. She decided that it was time for the foolproof insomnia remedy, which always seemed to work wonders for her during emotional emergencies. The idea was simple; during such crises Olivia simply got herself so physically exhausted by swimming, jogging or aerobics classes, that she was too tired to think. If tonight didn't qualify as a crisis, she didn't know what did.

She snapped off her light and moved stealthily, opening the door a crack and peering out into the hallway. Once her eyes became accustomed to the dark again, she could see Jonas's closed bedroom door. Olivia went quietly down the stairs.

Trying to be as quiet as humanly possible, she opened the back door and crept across the deck. Jonas's bedroom was directly above, and she only hoped he was not having the same difficulty sleeping.

The beach seemed darker than it had when she and Jonas had taken their walk. Then she realized that fewer lights were on in the houses along the shoreline. A soft blanket of mist had moved in over the area, making Olivia feel desolate and alone. Suddenly, out of the corner of her eye she saw something moving toward her. She spun around to find herself face-to-face with Jonas.

"What are you doing out here?"

"I might ask you the same thing. I thought you were asleep. You didn't answer when I knocked on your door before," he reminded her.

"I was already in the shower," she lied. He looked sad and it hurt her to think of him out here all alone, brooding. Even though that was exactly what she had come out here to do. "I couldn't sleep. I just came out for a little air."

"Me too." He was wearing a hooded sweatshirt and he dug his hands into its front pockets. Olivia had the feeling that he was trying to say something that was difficult for him. "I'm sorry about before. I didn't mean to pressure you like that about staying. That was wrong of me."

"You didn't pressure me," she said, thinking about the way he had taken her in his arms and kissed her. "Not exactly."

"You know what I mean. It's just that I want you so badly I can't even... Oh, damn. I'm doing it again." He shook his head and began to walk back toward the house. "Good night, Olivia," he called out over his shoulder. "I'll see you in the morning."

Olivia watched his broad back disappearing into the gloom. "Jonas? Jonas, wait a minute," she called after him.

He turned his head once to look at her but continued walking. Olivia trotted after him and grabbed hold of his arm.

"Jonas?"

"Olivia, you really don't know what you're doing," he said, staring straight ahead. "Unless you're about to tell me that you've changed your mind, I strongly suggest you let go of my arm."

Alarmed by his tone, Olivia didn't know what to do. The only thing she knew for sure was that she cared about him too much to let him go just then. "I'm not letting you go. I think we should talk."

He shook his head. "We've covered it all before, I think."

"You don't understand. It's just that I'm scared." He didn't respond. "I don't want you to leave like this." Olivia moved around in front of him and looked up into his face. She tried to catch his eye, but he looked away. "Hold me, Jonas," she said quietly. "Please."

At first he didn't move. Olivia held her breath. Then very slowly he took his hands from his pockets and opened his arms to her. She moved toward him and he drew her slim body into the circle of his warmth.

They were silent for a long time. Olivia locked her arms around his waist and pressed her cheek to his chest. She could hear his heart beating and the sound seemed to drown out the doubts that echoed in her mind. Jonas sighed into her hair.

"I've been wanting to hold you like this ever since I saw you out here."

"I'm glad you didn't walk away from me," she whispered.

"That's just the problem. I can't seem to leave you alone."

"And I can't leave you alone, either. At least not tomorrow."

It seemed to take a moment for the meaning of her words to sink in. Then Jonas pulled back and stared down into her eyes. He kissed her deeply, then cupped her cheek with one hand. "And there's still so much left of tonight. What do you propose we do with all that time...both of us unable to sleep for some odd reason.''

Olivia was silent for a moment. She knew that Jonas would accept whatever answer she chose to give him. She still had her doubts, but she needed to feel his love even more. "I think we should go back to the house," she said very slowly, "and you can show me the view from your room."

"Don't tease me, Olivia," he warned her in a husky whisper.

Without answering, she reached up and moved his head down toward her own, their lips meeting in a searing, passion-filled kiss.

Jonas was the first to pull away. With his arm firmly around Olivia's waist he set a swift pace across the beach and back to the house.

When they reached the back door, Olivia leaned over to brush the sand from her clothes, and suddenly found herself swept up in Jonas's arms.

"What in the world are you doing?" she asked, grasping him around the neck. "You'll hurt your back."

"It couldn't hurt worse than watching you dawdle in the doorway all night, lady," he whispered in her ear.

They were soon up the stairs, down the hall and into the bedroom. Jonas gently placed Olivia on the bed, but did not reach over to turn on the lights. "Wait here a second. Don't move an inch."

She could hear him fumbling in the dark and then the sound of a match being lit. Suddenly, the room was illuminated in the soft glow of a ceramic oil lamp on the dresser.

He turned to walk toward her and didn't take his eyes off her for an instant, one hand undoing the zipper of his sweatshirt.

Olivia slid over and reached up to help him. "Here, let me do that," she said, taking over the task.

Jonas placed his hands on her shoulders and Olivia could feel his grip tighten as she pressed her lips to the warm skin on his chest. She peeled his shirt back over his broad, hard shoulders and let her lips wander over the contours of his muscular physique. Her tongue swirled over one flat, masculine nipple and she could feel a shudder passing through his body. Finally, Jonas pulled back, took off the shirt and let it drop to the floor.

His arms circled her as he pulled her down to the bed beside him, his lips wandering hungrily over her face and neck. When he reached the edge of her sweatshirt, he fairly groaned with frustration. "Let me get this thing off you." Half-dazed with passion, she lifted her arms up and allowed Jonas to help her take it off. Hit by a rush of cold air, she suddenly remembered that it was all she had on and in a reflex motion her arms folded to cover her breasts.

Jonas's hands were soon on top of hers, gently unfolding her arms as he stared adoringly into her eyes. "Let me keep you warm, darling," he whispered as he moved down toward her. "I can't wait to feel you against me." He sighed, wrapping his arms around her. "You feel like heaven in my arms, Olivia. You always do. I never want to let you go." He sighed again as his mouth came down on hers.

And I never want you to, she answered silently as she felt her tongue twine deliciously with his.

His hands moved tenderly over her, eliciting electrifying sensations of pleasure wherever they touched. His kiss coaxed her passion to greater and greater heights as he gently teased her hardened nipple with his fingertips. Olivia felt herself rising on a crest of mindless delight as waves of maddening heat rippled through her limbs. Then Jonas's mouth moved from her lips to her neck, then across her smooth shoulder. His dark head finally dipped down to her breasts, his tongue flickering over their hardened tips.

When his mouth finally closed and slowly sucked one sensitive peak, Olivia sighed with pleasure. Her fingers twined in his hair as she felt the very core of her go molten with inexpressible desire.

"Sweetheart...you're so warm and responsive," he murmured, rising up slightly to softly cup both of her breasts in his hands. "Not to mention sexy—" he dipped his head down to kiss her lips "—and delicious." He kissed her deeply, circling her body with his strong embrace, the crisp, dark hair on his chest continuing to tease her sensitive breasts.

Olivia allowed her hands to roam freely across his bare torso, delighting in the feel of him, the play of muscle and warm flesh. Pulling her mouth away from his, she trailed her tongue seductively down the salty tasting column of his throat until he groaned with pleasure. It gave her a heady feeling of power to bring him so much pleasure. Yet, to Olivia, making love with Jonas tonight was not just an exercise in giving and receiving pleasure—it was an expression of emotions that came from deep within her very heart and soul. She wanted to please him, to make him happy in a hundred different ways, to show him how much she cared. She felt as if being with him tonight was very right and their lovemaking was exactly as it should be.

The weight of his body on hers was a pleasurable burden. She brushed her hands lovingly along the length of his back down to his hard lean flanks. "You feel wonderful against me," she said with a sigh.

"Olivia...can you feel what you're doing to me, honey?" He pressed his hips against hers in a primitive invitation and she could feel his hard, throbbing manhood against the soft, inner curve of her thigh. "I want you so much," he groaned against her hair.

Olivia could not remember when a man had made her feel more desirable, more passionate or more gloriously alive. She had never experienced anything like the sensual magic that happened each time she and Jonas touched. She had felt it again and again, all day long, when they had briefly kissed or just shared a special look. But nothing had quite prepared her for the full force of her feelings, the response that echoed to the very depths of her soul as she lay here beside him. Kissing him, holding him, running her hands over his body. Receiving exquisite pleasure from his touch and returning it in kind. It was a powerful, almost frightening feeling, and Olivia wanted very much to experience their special chemistry to the limit.

Wordlessly, he covered her face with enticingly sweet kisses as his hands pulled her jeans and panties down over her hips. With Olivia's help, Jonas slipped his shorts down over his legs and was soon lying beside her once more without a single thread separating their bare skin. His hands wandered hotly over her body, his fingertips finally sliding up between her thighs to the source of her femininity.

Olivia felt herself spiraling up, caught in a whirlpool of excitement as Jonas continued to stroke and tease her. She shivered with pleasure and clung fiercely to his huge shoulders, as wave after wave of pleasure broke over her.

"Jonas..." Finally she was able to speak.

"Hush, love," he soothed her, drawing her close to him again. "I want this to be perfect for you," he whispered in her ear.

"Jonas, please." She sighed against his mouth, angling her body beneath his. "Don't make me wait any longer...."

He entered her smoothly as she wrapped her legs around his waist and felt herself shudder at the first impact of his body. Jonas gathered her close, and they moved together as one in passion's age-old rhythm.

Matching the rhythm of Jonas's lovemaking, Olivia felt as if their bodies had melded into one, the exquisite pleasure of their union lifting them higher and higher, far above the material realm to a distant, indescribable place. A place where their souls were dancing as one toward a brilliant light, on the very brink of entering that light and bursting into flame.

Olivia felt herself unable to hold off the end another instant, carried over the edge in a fierce sensual
explosion. She held on to Jonas, burying her cheek
against his shoulder, and seconds later heard him call
out her name in a groan of ecstasy as his body tensed
with the climax of his pleasure.

They lay silently for some time, unable to speak or
even move. Jonas shifted his body beside her. Resting
his head next to hers on the pillow, he reached up and
idly stroked back her hair with one hand, the other
possessively clinging to her hip.

"You're beautiful to make love with," he said softly
with his eyes closed. "You couldn't turn your back on
what we have now so easily, could you?" he asked, his
eyes opening suddenly.

She turned her head on the pillow to look at him.
His tender gaze revealed a wealth of emotion, a vision that brought her both joy and fear. The feelings
she saw in Jonas's eyes, she knew were matched in her
own heart. The emotional involvement growing between them was much more than a casual affair.
"No...I couldn't," she admitted, reaching up to touch
his cheek.

Olivia fell asleep wrapped in Jonas's warm embrace. When she awoke, she was disoriented and
couldn't remember at first where she was. Slowly, a
recollection of the night's events returned to her and
she realized that she was alone. A clock on the night-
stand read 6:00 a.m. She got out of bed and pulled on
Jonas's shirt, which was lying on the floor. The door
to the deck was open and she walked toward it.

"Jonas?" He was standing at the deck's wooden railing, gazing out at the water, and turned to face her with a wide smile. He opened his arms to her and she moved toward him sleepily.

"My, my...you do wonders for that shirt, madam," he said, enfolding her in his arms. "I might just hide all your clothes and make you wear it for the rest of the weekend."

"It's very comfortable," Olivia said with a huge yawn. "Maybe I will. What are you doing up so early?"

He shrugged. "I don't know. Just thinking. Maybe my body just feels too good to sleep." His mouth curved in an intimate, teasing grin and Olivia felt herself beginning to blush.

"What were you thinking about?" Hooking her arms around his waist, she looked up at him. Badly in need of a shave, his hair tousled from the wind, in Olivia's eyes he was the most fantastically attractive man she had ever seen.

"Oh, just about you and me," he slowly admitted, "and what looks like another gorgeous day. So, do you like the view from this room at sunrise?"

"It's everything you said it would be." Olivia smiled up at him. "I'm very impressed."

With his arms encircling her waist, Jonas pulled her closer. Through the thin fabric of his shorts, she could feel his growing desire. "Just what a man likes to hear the morning after, sweetheart. Come back into the bedroom with me and I'll impress you some more."

Six

Have you gone crazy?'' Jonas put down his mug of coffee and stared at her. ''Did you fall down in the shower and hit your head?''

''I know it's difficult to believe, but I'm honestly not joking. When you call Marsha and Brad this morning, I want you to invite them here as we had originally planned.''

''Correction. As *I* had originally planned and as you had protested to violently, going so far as to throw heavy objects across your hotel room at me in order to express your displeasure.''

Olivia sighed, recalling the scene. Jonas was partly correct with his shower theory. The thought had come to her just moments ago while washing up, but she'd never guessed that he'd be so adamantly opposed to the idea. His firm objections, however, only caused Olivia to be all the more determined to have her way. They served to convince her for once and for all that Jonas's interest in her was sincere and without ulterior motivation. The more Olivia mulled it over, the more convinced she became that Jonas had tossed away the biggest business prospect of his career on the slim hope that their mutual attraction would eventually evolve into something more. Knowing that any curiosity at all regarding Brad's business would cast his interest in her in a suspicious light, Jonas had nobly turned his back on the Multi-Foods account for Olivia's sake. He truly was a romantic in the Renaissance tradition, bona fide scholar or not.

Olivia felt personally responsible for taking this lifetime chance away from him. Why couldn't they do it? she had wondered upstairs. To say that she cared about him a great deal would be stating the case only mildly. She couldn't quite admit it to herself, but in her unguarded moments she realized that she was falling in love with him. His concerns had suddenly become her concerns. Seeing him happy would make her happy. There was very little she could think of that she would not do to help him. If pretending to be his wife for two days would enable him to walk off with the pot full of gold at the end of Madison Avenue's rainbow, then she would do it. Ironically, her only obstacle was Jonas.

"Why in the world are you looking at me like that? I thought you had enough of playing Mrs. Jonas Harper to last a lifetime."

His offhand statement had struck a sensitive chord in Olivia this morning. Now she could very well consider taking on the role for life, and the thought scared her. "I'm just trying to help you," she answered lightly, "but I can see that you're too damn stubborn to know what's good for you."

"I certainly do know what's good for me. I decided to chase after you instead of Brad Carmichael, didn't I?"

"That's just what I mean, Jonas. In your mind you made some kind of conscious choice between getting to know me, or going after that business deal." Olivia looked down at her napkin, which she twisted and retwisted between her fingers as she spoke. "I think that was very sweet of you...really," she said hesitantly. "I probably wouldn't have come here at all if I'd even suspected it was any different. But that's not a problem anymore. I know you better now and...I don't want this to be a problem for us later," she finally admitted in a quiet rush of words.

Jonas stared at her thoughtfully, his expression yielding little clue to his feelings. She wondered if she had made the slightest dent in his stubborn convictions.

"Well, I'm glad to hear that you at least think we might have a 'later' to worry about," he said finally. Then sighed. "So you think I might have some regrets down the road, do you?"

"Possibly, if there is a down the road."

"There will be one. You'd better count on it," he replied sharply. "And I know I won't have any second thoughts about all of this, Olivia. Believe me."

"I believe that you mean it now, but who can really say for sure? I don't want to think I've taken anything away from you, don't you understand that? It's only for two days, Jonas. Won't you just do it for me? Please?" She reached out and took his hand. She tried to catch his gaze, but he continued staring down at his plate.

"I'm not saying that I agree with you," he said slowly, "but if you're that worried about it, I suppose we could give it a try."

Olivia really wasn't quite as worried as she had made it seem. She didn't think Jonas was the type of man who looked back with regrets about things he should or shouldn't have done. But the argument had been a clever way to get him to agree to entertaining the Carmichaels, as planned, she silently congratulated herself.

"Good, I'm glad you're finally coming to your senses about this whole thing. At least this time we'll have a chance to plan things out a little and get our story straight."

"I doubt if we could ever get our story straight," Jonas said with some dismay. "The best we can shoot for is to get them so distracted that they won't notice."

"Now, now," she admonished him. "If you're going to be so pessimistic about this whole thing we won't have a chance at pulling off the typical-cozy-couple routine.''

He smiled slyly at her. "You know I can do the 'cozy' part in my sleep. It's the other part I worry about. It seems to me that nothing we do together is exactly 'typical.' ''

"Don't split hairs, Jonas. I think you better get on the phone and call them," she said, glancing at her watch. "Then get out that paella recipe. I'd better start studying up on it right away."

Jonas looked up at the sky with an expression of dismay. "What have I done here? I've created a monster," he moaned.

"I think you'd better call, before they make other plans, Jonas," she said sweetly

Jonas rose from his seat with some reluctance and headed toward the bright red kitchen wall phone. "Yes, Olivia dear... whatever *you* say, dear," he replied in a nasal-pitched imitation of a henpecked husband.

"Now you're getting the idea." She smiled smugly as she began to clear away their breakfast dishes. "And don't take long with that call. We've got a lot of work to do around here before they arrive."

Jonas's deep-sounding, voluble groan suddenly turned into a coughing sound. "Oh, hello there, Brad. I—uh—didn't hear you come on the line. This is Jonas Harper. Seems to be some trouble with the connection," he ad-libbed, "Oh... I can hear you fine now...."

Dumping the dishes in the sink, Olivia tried to stifle her laughter. "Let the games begin," she whispered to herself.

The rest of their morning was devoted to preparing the house for their guests, who were due to arrive early in the afternoon. The first order of business was fixing up the guest room. Jonas eagerly volunteered to move all of Olivia's things into his bedroom and then returned to help her change the bed linen and straighten up the bathroom. They tidied up the rest of the house, and at Jonas's suggestion Olivia tossed some of her paperbacks and scripts around the living room for effect.

Next, like any other married couple preparing for houseguests, they discussed the menu for the next few days and made up a shopping list. Olivia, of course, left most of this task to Jonas since his culinary skills were infinitely superior to her own. However, she was able to toss in a few good ideas for side dishes and desserts. Though she hated to cook, she certainly was never at a loss to think of delicious things she'd like to eat.

When the list was complete, they jumped into the car and raced over to the supermarket. Olivia wheeled the cart while Jonas took charge of the list with utmost concentration and seriousness. It was something like watching Michelangelo choose pieces of marble for his sculptures, Olivia decided as she watched Jonas thoughtfully squeeze tomatoes and sniff melons in the fresh produce department.

They were next to a bin of squash when Jonas looked up at her very seriously. "I bet you don't even know that some of these vegetables are male and some are female."

"Don't be silly, Jonas. Of course I know that. In fact, most men I've dated lately fall into the vegetable category."

"Well it matters when you're cooking," he said, ignoring her glib remark as he sifted through a pile of eggplant and finally made his choice. "Especially with eggplant."

Olivia smiled at him. "I can see that you're very serious about this, Jonas. For a minute there, I thought you were just trying to talk sexy to me right here in the produce section."

Jonas stepped up beside her and, putting his arm around her waist, gave her his full and undivided attention for the first time since they had entered the store. "Never in produce. I was holding off until we got to the aisle with the chocolate syrup," he whispered in her ear.

"That sounds very decadent and fattening."

"Worth every calorie, I assure you," he promised.

Olivia turned and smiled at him. He was wearing a Cheshire cat grin, his eyes sparkling merrily. It was amazing how easily he was able to make her pulse quicken. She felt like a kid with a schoolgirl crush.

"On to the onions," she said, pushing the cart forward. "White or red?"

* * *

Back at the house, with the groceries put away and the stage set, there was little to do but wait for the Carmichaels' arrival.

"What do you think I should be doing when they get here, Jonas? Reading one of these magazines, maybe?" Olivia held up one of the many house and garden periodicals she had grabbed off the rack at the checkout counter. "Or maybe I should be darning your socks or something."

"Darning my socks? Don't be ridiculous. We're not trying out for the Ozzie and Harriet award here. Just be yourself, for heaven's sake."

That was just the problem. Olivia worried that at close hand and prolonged scrutiny she could never pass herself off as a married person. "What about pet names?"

"Pet names?" he echoed in a puzzled voice. "You mean like Rover and Spot?"

"For each other, silly. Married people always have little nicknames for each other, didn't you ever notice?"

"Oh, you mean like Snookums and Bunny-buns and that sort of thing?"

"Well, we don't have to go overboard with this. It was only a suggestion." Olivia restlessly tossed aside her decorating magazine and rose off the chaise longue.

"Or Pookie-pie and Sugar-lamb?" he continued to provoke her with a teasing grin.

"Jonas..." she began in a warning tone. But before she could finish her sentence, the front doorbell sounded, shocking them both for an instant into speechlessness.

"I think our guests have arrived," Jonas said finally, getting up from his chair and quickly running his hand through his hair. "Why don't we go greet them together...Honey-bear?"

Scowling, Olivia swept past him and headed for the front door. Her expression was all smiles, however, as she greeted Marsha and Brad, ushering them in with Jonas right beside her.

"Oh, the house is just gorgeous," Marsha said with a sigh as she surveyed her surroundings. "I just love what you've done with it, Olivia."

"Why, thank you." Olivia beamed. "I tried for that Southwestern uncluttered look," she explained, quoting from the magazine she had just leafed through.

"Well, you really do have a marvelous eye for color," Brad went on.

"It takes time to get everything just the way you want it in a house this size, of course, but I do enjoy paging through magazines and getting ideas," Olivia graciously replied.

Behind Brad's and Marsha's backs, Olivia could see Jonas's eyes widen as he shook his head. The expression on his face was for Olivia's eyes only, and it was one that only she could understand. "I think I'll just go out and grab the luggage, give the car that *uncluttered* look," he mumbled, excusing himself.

Marsha smiled at him briefly, hardly aware of his exit as she studied a piece of Indian pottery. Olivia suddenly wondered if Jonas regretted taking up their charade again. Here she was, trying to do something nice for him, and he didn't seem to appreciate it.

"Wait for me now, Jonas. I won't have you spoiling us while we're out here," Brad warned in a friendly tone as he trailed after his host.

"Why don't I show you the guest room and you can get changed for the beach. Then we'll have some lunch," Olivia said, leading Marsha upstairs. This was not going to be easy, she realized, smiling widely at her guest, not easy at all.

When Jonas caught up with her a short while later, Olivia was in the kitchen, assembling the ingredients for lunch and preparing to set the table out on the deck.

"Well, we're ten minutes into this thing. Only forty-seven hours and fifty minutes, approximately, to go." Jonas chomped down on a carrot she had cleaned and washed for the salad.

"I think it's going fine so far," she said in a hushed tone. "What do you think?"

"You're the hostess with the mostest, dear," he replied dryly.

"Jonas, if you didn't want to go through with this, you really should have told me," she said in the same hushed, but far more urgent manner. "I just don't understand what's bothering you."

Jonas said nothing, pulling on his apron and taking over the cooking with a grim look on his handsome face. "I know that you're going to all this trouble for my sake, Olivia, and it's not that I don't appreciate it but—business or no business—I much preferred having you all to myself out here, quite frankly," he whispered back. "I guess I didn't realize until they showed up that now we'll have so little time to ourselves before you have to go." He took an onion she had cleaned and started chopping it mercilessly on a wooden block.

"Why, Jonas, that's so sweet." Olivia walked over to him and put her arms around his waist.

"Well, it's true," he said. He looked down at her, his grouchiness somewhat dispelled by her attentions. "You don't have to get all teary-eyed about it." He put down the knife and put his arms around her in a comforting embrace.

"I'm not...it's just the onions," she said, not willing to admit that the onions weren't totally to blame for the dampness around her eyes. "I guess I didn't think of that part."

He smiled at her. "We'll make up for it tonight," he promised, lifting her face toward his. His warm lips came down on hers, and Olivia slipped her arms around his back to hold him closer.

Their kiss began to deepen, and already she could feel the powerful effect her slightest touch seemed to have on Jonas. "Hmm...sweetheart. You don't know what you do to me," he said, sighing. "I could make love to you right here and now."

Olivia was just about to reply to his scandalous but almost irresistible invitation when she heard footsteps coming through the kitchen doorway. Her eyes flew open to find Brad, looking almost as embarrassed as she felt.

"Oh—sorry. I was just looking for something to drink. A glass of water maybe?" he stammered, looking from Olivia to Jonas as he began to back out of the kitchen.

"Ice water?" Olivia asked, breaking free of Jonas's embrace. "Coming right up," she said, bustling around the kitchen. "Why don't you wait on the deck and I'll bring it out for you?" she offered.

Glad to escape the awkward situation, Brad smiled and slipped outside. With a sigh, Jonas seized his knife and took up chopping the onion once again with a vengeance.

All things considered the afternoon with Marsha and Brad went surprisingly well. There were a few moments when Olivia and Jonas got their signals crossed, but they were easily smoothed over. It was becoming frighteningly easy to play the role of Mrs. Jonas Harper, Olivia realized. Somehow the thought made her feel warm and pleasant inside, but wary of what the future might hold, as well.

After one of Jonas's gourmet lunches, the four of them stretched out on the beach for some sun, swam and then played Frisbee touch football. Even Zeke joined in—although neither team seemed willing to claim him as their own.

When Olivia had met Marsha in San Diego she could only recall all the negative aspects of their former relationship. But as this day wore on, she began to remember why they had been such close friends all those years ago. Marsha was vivacious, bright and certainly fun to be around. She had a way of handling herself just right in any social situation, which was a trait Olivia had always admired. She could see now that the poise and reserve Marsha had possessed as a young woman had been honed and polished to perfection over the years. She was a sophisticated, interesting woman who could converse on almost any subject—art, the theater, politics—and Olivia had to admit that she was inspired with a renewed respect for her girlhood friend. Not only respect, but the rekindling of affection as well.

Olivia had come to see the unhappiness that had passed between them as a fateful event that had altered their lives for the best. There was no doubt in Olivia's mind that Marsha was the perfect wife for a man like Brad. Seeing them again only served to reaffirm her belief that marrying Brad would have only caused unhappiness for them both.

Olivia's feelings toward Brad were a bit more complex. In college their age difference of four years had seemed much greater to her. She was a naive, unsophisticated girl and Brad was her first steady boyfriend. It had seemed to her then that he knew practically everything. He had already completed his graduate degree in business and had been out in the real working world. She still wondered now what he had seen in her—though she supposed that to a man in his early twenties such unquestioning adoration from a beautiful young woman did have its appeal. Little by little, she had begun to find her independent nature bending to Brad's preferences. She'd dressed for him, had worn her hair the way he like it, had talked, walked and even acted the way she thought he wanted her to. At least, at first she had until her strong need for self-expression had overwhelmed her desire for Brad's approval.

It had shown itself in little ways at first, petty arguments about nothing at all, such as Olivia deciding to wear a pair of outlandish earrings or an outfit she knew Brad hated. It was during the winter of her senior year and she had known somehow that their plans just weren't going to work out. But her youth and inexperience had prevented her from taking any action on her doubts. She wondered if her worries were just a normal phase for two people contemplating marriage. She often assured herself that once she graduated and they began a real life together, everything would smooth out somehow.

In the meantime, as spring approached, Brad and Marsha had begun to spend more and more time together. At first, it was purely accidental—or at least, seemed so—when Olivia would find Brad waiting for her to return from the library, or from practicing a scene with another acting student. It had hardly seemed strange that Marsha had made him a cup of coffee and put on the stereo they shared in their dorm room. At first, Olivia had thought nothing of it and had been glad in fact that the two people closest to her got along so well.

That March, she had won a lead role in a campus production of *A Streetcar Named Desire*. She was cast to play Blanche Dubois, a part that required a tremendous amount of study and concentration. Rehearsals had seemed to absorb all of her spare time and Brad was not at all understanding when Olivia had to cancel their regular weekend dates and squeeze in meetings at haphazard breaks in her schedule. He disapproved of her interest in acting and disliked all of the people she associated with.

On sunny Saturdays and Sundays, while Olivia was stuck in a dark, musty auditorium, relying on "the kindness of strangers," what was poor neglected Brad to do with himself? He had been trying in vain to teach Olivia how to play tennis, a game she could never quite get the hang of. Marsha, with her country club upbringing, was an excellent tennis player and could also hold her own on the golf course, when pressed upon to do so. Olivia could still recall the morning she had arranged the first real date between her best friend and her fiancé. She could even remember how grateful she had been to Marsha for taking Brad out on the tennis courts while she was preparing for stardom.

Inevitably, one thing had led to another with Marsha and Brad. From tennis dates, to the movies, to a host of other casual get-togethers that became gradually less and less platonic. Opening night of Olivia's play arrived and naturally, Marsha and Brad had front row seats for the performance. Olivia stood in the wings, waiting for her first entrance. She peeked out from behind the curtain, past the footlights and found

Marsha and Brad sitting side by side. They weren't holding hands, barely glancing at each other in fact, but even at that distance she could see that it wasn't just her best friend and fiancé sitting there, but an attractive young couple in love. The realization was stunning. Somehow she had moved out onstage at the appropriate moment, and another force took over. Later, everyone had congratulated her on a stirring performance, but she could barely remember a moment of it.

Brad and Marsha brought roses backstage, and they all went out to a lavish dinner at the fanciest restaurant in town. Olivia did not confront either of them with her suspicions. Instead, weeks later, she allowed Brad to take her out for a long drive and sat silently as he struggled through an explanation of his change of heart. She felt crushed and humiliated, but was also somehow strangely relieved that the problem was finally out in the open.

The showdown had been just days before her graduation ceremony. Under some trumped-up excuse, Marsha had already moved her belongings back to her parents' home. Olivia took her diploma and went back to the house in Tuckahoe to lick her wounds and listen to her grandmother bad-mouth both Brad and Marsha in a most witty and comforting way. After a few months, Brad and Marsha had each tried to reconcile with Olivia, but she had already moved to Manhattan to try her luck with thousands of other fledgling actors and actresses. She had tossed out their letters unread, determined to put the past completely behind her.

Throughout this day, she occasionally caught Brad looking at her, and she wondered if he was reviewing the events of the past, as she was. He was attentive to her, complimenting her every chance he had and joking with her in an easy, sociable way. She had the oddest feeling at times that he was still attracted to her, but brushed this thought out of her mind as completely outlandish. It was more likely, she thought, that he still felt guilty for having jilted her for Marsha and was now trying to make it up to her in some way. She certainly no longer regarded him as the last word in urbane, worldly sophistication. She could more than hold her own with him and that knowledge gave her a good feeling. She tried her best to make him feel comfortable and welcome in Jonas's home.

She honestly didn't care what Brad thought about her, but she didn't want any sour feelings from their old ties to affect his relationship with Jonas. After all, she was putting herself through all of this for Jonas's sake, wasn't she?

It was late in the day when Marsha suggested that she and Olivia take a walk down the beach. Brad and Jonas were sitting on the deck, discussing business, and Olivia fervently hoped that Jonas was making some headway with the excellent advertising ideas he had told her about that morning. She decided that a brisk walk was just the thing she needed to work off some of the restless energy she felt every time she saw the two men chatting together.

"It was so nice of you to invite us out here," Marsha began as they walked along the beach. "You can't imagine how badly Brad needed this break. Sometimes his schedule on these business trips gets so hectic I don't know what to do to get him to slow down. Do you have the same problem with Jonas?"

Oh, no, Olivia thought nervously, here comes the wife-to-wife girl talk. "Jonas? Just the same. He can just keep on going and going . . . if he really gets excited about something," she said, thinking more about his all-night lovemaking than anything that even vaguely had to do with business. "In fact, I've never met a man before with quite so much . . . energy," she confessed.

"Really? What's his secret?"

"He really just adores what he's doing, I guess." Olivia smiled. "Takes a lot of vitamins, too," she added as an afterthought.

"Well, he's quite a guy," Marsha replied. "I know it couldn't have been all that easy for either of you, going out of your way to have us here like this."

So, the cat's finally out of the bag, Olivia thought. "The past is past for me," she said honestly. "I don't hold any grudges. I think it all happened for the best, if you really want to know the truth."

"Do you really?" Marsha asked, plainly surprised by this admission. "I mean—I've always felt that way myself, but I never imagined that you did, too. Unless you're just saying this to make me feel better."

Olivia shook her head. "Of course not. I think you and Brad are a perfect match. I never would have made a good wife for him, that's for sure."

"You? Not make a good wife for Brad? Olivia, how could you say that? Why, when I was first getting to know Brad, I always felt as if he was comparing us both and that I was so inadequate next to you. I was more surprised than anyone when he told me that he wanted to break off his engagement and marry me. I was in love with him...I think maybe I was even before he had ever noticed I was alive. But I really thought he was only using me to make you jealous. You know, I was always so envious of you," Marsha confessed, "I thought you were just about perfect, everything I ever wanted to be."

"You thought I was perfect?" Now it was Olivia's turn to be shocked. "But you were the perfect one, Marsha. Not me. You had the right upbringing, the right clothes—you were so smart and popular. You were always such a class act. Even back then."

"Oh, my parents made sure their little Dallas princess had a respectable amount of cashmere sweaters and knew how to treat a maître d' with the proper air of disdain...but my upbringing and family life seemed just so boring compared to yours, Livy," she said, using the nickname Olivia hadn't heard for years. "Why, if you had been raised by a band of Gypsies, I couldn't have found you any more interesting. You were never programmed by a crowd of people, telling you what to do or think. Forcing you always to do the proper thing. Oh, maybe you were a trifle shy at times, but you were really your own person. I always loved that about you ... I would have traded ten of my Neiman Marcus wardrobes for the unpolished, free-spirited style you had about you."

"I never thought of it like that." Olivia kicked a chunk of sand with her toe. "You always seemed so confident and sure of yourself."

"I guess I did act that way, but I was really very insecure. I suppose that was part of the reason I tried to attract Brad's attention in the first place. In some stupid, schoolgirl way I guess I thought that if I could get him away from you, it would mean that I was really as attractive and interesting as you were." Marsha gave a long sigh and Olivia could tell that even after all this time it had been a difficult admission for her to make. "I still feel pretty awful about the whole thing. I can't tell you how sorry I am about the way I betrayed you. You should really still hate me. How can you forgive me for being such a despicable friend?"

Olivia stopped walking and looked at Marsha. She had never really considered the other side of the story. She had never imagined that, in a strange way, Marsha's interest in Brad had in fact stemmed from her admiration for Olivia. She had never suspected that the woman continued to feel guilty and remorseful to this day.

Finally, she reached out and patted Marsha's arm. "Of course I don't hate you. You know, you're really not the only one to blame. I had as a big a part in the whole mess as anyone." Marsha tried to interrupt, but Olivia stopped her. "No, hear me out. I've given it all some thought since I ran into you the other day. I knew things weren't right between Brad and me, but I guess I just didn't want to deal with it.'' She shrugged. ''Let's face it, I practically threw him at you. Now I can see that I really wanted a way out of that engagement, but back then, I just couldn't be the first one to rock the boat. We were all so very young. Please don't feel badly about it anymore, Marsha. I forgave you a very long time ago.''

Marsha's wide blue eyes were shining and for a moment Olivia thought she was going to cry. Ever poised and discreet, however, she got hold of herself and just smiled, reaching out to squeeze Olivia's hand. ''It hasn't been hard for me to remember why we were such an inseparable pair back then, Olivia.''

''Not for me, either,'' Olivia replied with a smile. ''Not counting the stolen boyfriends, of course,'' she teased.

Marsha laughed. ''You and Jonas look so happy together. I bet you haven't given any of this a thought for years.''

''Uh, well, you could say that meeting Jonas has put everything in a new perspective for me.''

''I was really very happy to hear that you had gotten married, Olivia. Just my guilt acting up, I suppose. Then when I met Jonas . . . well, I'm sure you don't need to be told that he's quite a catch. And so attentive to you . . . Anyone would say you two had just met, instead of being an old married couple like the rest of us.''

"Amazing as it may sound, we're still getting to know each other," Olivia said wistfully.

"He's so charming, isn't he?" Marsha laughed. "It's funny the way things work out. Maybe you and Jonas were just fated to fall in love and get married all along. We can't fight destiny, can we?"

"Marsha, at this point," Olivia said solemnly, "I wouldn't even dream of trying."

Olivia felt her smile slipping ever so slightly as they turned and headed back toward the house. Marsha's prophetic commentary had hit a little too close to home. These days, Olivia seemed powerless to oppose the forces that seemed to be drawing her closer and closer to Jonas. If it was destiny at work, then she was beginning to think that she might as well just surrender.

When they returned to the house, Marsha and Brad retired to their room while Olivia joined Jonas in the kitchen. It was time to begin preparing the famous paella, and Olivia was almost looking forward to another fun-filled cooking lesson from Jonas. But from the onset, she could see that dinner preparations tonight were not going to resemble in the least the leisurely comedy of errors that had taken place in the kitchen the night before. Jonas took charge of his domain like a general preparing for battle. Olivia felt her patience stretched to the limit as she hustled to and fro, completing her assigned duties as official cook's helper.

"How did your discussion with Brad go?" she asked casually after they had been working in silence for quite some time.

"Very good—well, better than good, great actually. He went wild over the preliminary ideas I showed him. He's asked me to do a full presentation in San Francisco as soon as possible."

"That's fantastic," Olivia said gleefully. She looked over at him. "Why don't you sound happy about this, Jonas? I would have thought you'd be doing handsprings around the house by now."

He shrugged. "I'll be happy when this is all over. When you and I are alone together again and we can take up where we left off. Then we'll have our own private celebration."

"Don't worry, Jonas," she said sympathetically. "It will all be over soon and everything will turn out just as we planned," she assured him.

Jonas shook his head in a worried manner as he stirred up a huge pot of saffron-colored rice. "I don't know. I just have this feeling that something's going to go wrong."

"They have to leave for Los Angeles tomorrow. What could go wrong?"

"I can't put my finger on it exactly," Jonas grumbled. "Maybe I just don't care for the way Brad's been eyeing you all day," he finally admitted.

"Brad? Oh, don't be silly. I think he's just trying to remember what he ever saw in me ten years ago, that's all. You don't think he suspects something, do you,

Jonas? I've tried to act as wifely as possible. Maybe I've been missing some cues.''

"You've hit all the right bases," he assured her. "A few that I didn't even know were there," he mumbled more to himself than her. He sighed audibly. "Just forget I said anything, okay? You're right, they're leaving tomorrow. What could go wrong?''

"That's the spirit." Olivia watched him out of the corner of her eye. Something was troubling him, a problem that he didn't feel quite ready to confide in her. She wondered now if his talk with Brad had really gone quite as well as he had described. She couldn't imagine Jonas lying to her about something like that. What purpose would it serve? But if he wasn't worried about business, she really couldn't guess exactly what was nettling him.

"How about a glass of wine, Jonas?" she suggested. "It will help you cook better.''

"Where did you pick up that tip? One of those home and garden magazines you were studying?''

"Now, now, don't be mean." She took him by the hand and all but pushed him down into a kitchen chair.

"I suppose I could sit for a minute," he said, taking the glass of white wine she poured for him. "Just make sure I don't drink too much of this stuff.''

"Don't worry, I can take over for you in a pinch," she said smugly, pouring herself a glass of wine also.

"You'll finish cooking dinner all by yourself, will you?" He reached out and pulled her into his lap. "This I'd like to see.''

"This is a fancy neighborhood. I'm sure I could just call up some Spanish restaurant and have a truckload of paella on your doorstep in no time." Olivia took a sip of her wine and then put her arms around his neck. "Just think of all the spare time we'd have on our hands."

"Taking the lazy way out would have its advantages," he said, nibbling her earlobe in a way that sent electric vibrations up and down Olivia's spine. "And I for one can certainly think of a lot of things I'd rather be doing right now than stirring up a pot of rice."

She slipped off his lap and untied her apron. "For instance?" she asked innocently.

He rose and gently took her by the hand to lead her out of the kitchen. "Frankly, I'd rather show you than tell you."

"But what about dinner, Jonas?" she asked, looking back over her shoulder at the pots of food. "How long can it stay like that?"

He glanced over at her with a devilish smile as he ushered her up the stairway. "As long as it takes, sweetheart. Just as long as it takes...."

Without exchanging another word, they walked quietly past the guest room and into the master bedroom. Once they were behind the solidly closed door, Olivia felt as if they had retreated into a world all their own.

Jonas walked across the room toward her and she willingly slipped into his arms. They didn't speak or even kiss for a very long moment, they simply held each other close, savoring the sensation of their bodies touching from head to toe.

"You feel so good in my arms. It feels like days since I held you like this." Jonas sighed.

Olivia felt too wonderful to answer him. It was only hours since they had been alone together, but she felt the same way Jonas did.

"I've been working you to death in the kitchen," he said remorsefully. "I think we could both use a dip in the whirlpool before dinner. How does that sound?" he whispered in her ear.

"If you plan on being in the same tub, I don't know how relaxing it's going to be," she answered honestly.

Jonas released her and ducked into the bathroom. "I'll take that as a compliment," he said over the sound of running water. "Relaxing or not, I'll guarantee you that you'll feel good all over after this."

"Or I'll drown smiling," she whispered to herself as she undressed and pinned up her hair. Wrapped in a towel, she entered the bathroom where Jonas was already immersed up to chest level in the steaming, swirling water. He sighed appreciatively as he stretched out his legs under the bubbling current. The tub was about four feet high and just as wide, set in a special alcove of the bathroom beneath a skylight and surrounded by wide-leafed tropical-looking plants. "My own private Eden," he said. "Come on in, the water's fine."

Olivia stepped toward the tub, unhooked her towel and began to climb in.

"Here, let me help you," he said, rising to lend her a hand. "Getting in can be a bit tricky."

I suppose you've had plenty of experience... helping women into this ceramic sin-bin, she wanted to say. "Have you had to increase your home insurance since getting this installed?" she asked sweetly.

Jonas laughed. "Do I detect a note of jealousy in your lovely voice, Olivia?" He tickled the tip of her nose with a loofah sponge.

"Me? Jealous? Don't be ridiculous," she scoffed.

"Well, just to set the record straight... this house has always been a very special place to me, and I haven't invited anyone to spend the weekend here in a very long time. Since before I had this tub installed, in fact," he added thoughtfully. "So I guess you could say you're my first, Olivia." He slid closer to her along the bench seat and held her close. "What do you say to that, wise guy?"

She looked at him very seriously and held his face between her hands. "Don't worry, Jonas, I'll be gentle with you," she teased him.

With a gruff sound in the back of his throat, he pulled her roughly toward him and Olivia knew that there was no holding back their longing for each other for another moment. They teased and taunted each other in the foamy water until their passion had built to a fevered pitch. Then, wrapped in huge, fluffy towels, they stretched out on Jonas's wide bed and the magic of their lovemaking continued to lift them to the stars and beyond.

As they lay together in the afterglow of ecstasy, Olivia realized that she had never felt closer or more in tune with anyone in her entire life. The loving rapport that had developed so quickly between them was as rare as it was precious. How had she managed without Jonas in her life? She'd only met him a few days ago, but at that moment, she couldn't seem to remember what her life was like before that. How would she manage without him, she wondered, when it was finally time for her to go back East?

Their heads lay together on the same pillow and she silently watched him sleep. Finally, he opened his eyes slowly and favored her with a drowsy, one-dimpled smile.

"So... pretty good for my first time, don't you think?" he asked in a smugly satisfied male way.

"Oh, I don't know." She ran one fingertip through the dark hair on his chest. "Might have just been beginner's luck," she said sagely.

"Beginner's luck, huh?" He sat up and smoothed the sheet out over his chest. "Well, maybe we should try again later, just to make sure."

"Maybe we should," she said, moving her mouth closer to his and sealing her promise with a kiss.

A short time later, Olivia and Jonas were dressed and downstairs, awaiting the entrance of their houseguests. Lighting the tall white candles on the dining room table, they looked the perfect picture of a successful young married couple entertaining at home. The table was set with Jonas's finest china and crys-

tal. Olivia had put the finishing touch to the table setting by arranging some freshly cut roses in a silver
bowl for the centerpiece.

"Isn't this lovely!" Brad entered the dining room,
looking fresh and relaxed from his shower and nap.
He was dressed in tan linen trousers and a pale yellow
cotton pullover sweater. His aviator-framed glasses
which he hadn't worn in college made him look dis-
tinguished. With his even tan and golden hair, he appeared every inch the successful, self-assured man in
his prime. Yet she could honestly say that she no
longer found him the least bit attractive. The only
feelings Brad now inspired in her were those of
friendship and perhaps a touch of nostalgia.

"Something smells delicious in here," Brad said,
sliding up alongside Olivia.

"It's paella," she replied.

He sniffed the air theatrically while one hand slid
lightly around her waist. "No, I don't think it's paella.
I'm almost positive it's my lovely hostess," he said
smoothly. "What is that perfume you're wearing,
Olivia? It's really quite exotic."

Suddenly Jonas was right beside them, breaking
into their intimate tête-à-tête. "Just her dandruff
shampoo, Brad. Nothing exotic about it. I'll give you
a bottle to take home if you like," he offered gener-
ously. "How about a drink before dinner?" Patting
Brad almost too heartily on the back, he steered his
guest away from Olivia and into the living room.

Feeling a bit perplexed, Olivia followed. She knew
that they were coming into the home stretch, but she

had the distinct feeling that this was going to be a very long evening.

Although Jonas and Brad had seemed to get along famously all day, Olivia now sensed a certain subtle tension between them. Even though Brad had reacted most favorably to Jonas's ideas, she had to remind herself that the deal wasn't signed, sealed and delivered. Certainly, this unanswered issue was on both of their minds. Unfortunately, Olivia noticed, Jonas seemed to be acting considerably cooler toward Brad as the night wore on. Perhaps he didn't want Brad to feel smothered with attention. But there was no sense causing bad feelings with Brad, either, just because Jonas had a case of the nerves.

Because of her concerns, Olivia made a special effort to take up Jonas's slack, being particularly attentive to her former flame throughout the evening. The more Jonas ignored him, the more of a special effort she made. She sat next to Brad at dinner, and asked him questions about his business and other interests such as golf and fishing. He never seemed to tire of talking about these hobbies, though the other three certainly had heard enough about them. Olivia considered it just part of her evening's performance. In fact, she tried her best to take some pointers from Marsha, who had a special knack for keeping the conversation at dinner afloat. A talent that Olivia suspected Marsha had perfected after years of accompanying Brad on occasions such as this one—a precarious mix of business and pleasure.

Just as Jonas had predicted, the paella was a great success and had not suffered in the least from an hour or two of neglect by the chef. Marsha asked for the recipe no less than three times and Brad eagerly accepted a second helping.

After dinner, the four of them moved to the deck for coffee, dessert and after-dinner drinks. It was a clear, warm night and as she gazed up into the star-studded sky, Olivia secretly thanked the powers above for helping her and Jonas carry off their little deception so smoothly.

Jonas reached over from where he sat and squeezed her hand. She had the strangest feeling that he had been thinking the same thing.

"Goodness, look at the time! It's already past one," Marsha said, glancing down at her watch. "I think we had better call it an evening. You did say we had to be in L.A. by noon tomorrow, Brad," she reminded her husband.

"So I did." He sighed, reluctant to move from his comfortable chair. "Some brunch meeting with a venture capitalist group. I've tried to put them off, but they've been after me for months to do something with their money," he explained in a weary tone. "I'd much rather spend the afternoon tossing around that Frisbee again with you folks. I can't tell you what a pleasure it's been coming out here—making new friends," he said, glancing warmly at Jonas, "and catching up with old friends, too," he concluded, his gaze turning toward Olivia.

"That's very sweet of you, Brad," Olivia replied. "We both wish you and Marsha could stay longer too—"

"But we certainly understand that business comes first," Jonas chimed in. "A man doesn't get to your position by choosing a game of Frisbee football over brunch with venture capitalists."

"I suppose you're right," Brad said wistfully. "But maybe you'll invite us out here again soon."

"Now darling, where are your manners? Olivia and Jonas have to visit us first in San Francisco for the weekend," Marsha insisted. "It's our turn to show them a great time."

Except for a terribly strained smile, Olivia could supply no response to Marsha's invitation. Luckily, Marsha hadn't really expected any, and after a few more pleasantries were exchanged, Marsha and Brad went upstairs. Olivia and Jonas were left alone in the kitchen to clear up the dishes. Jonas was strangely quiet and Olivia decided that the strain of the whole situation had finally gotten to him. Men were the weaker sex, after all, even though they put up a good show at times.

"Why don't you go on upstairs and I'll take care of the rest of this?" he offered.

"Don't be silly, Jonas. We'll finish it up together."

"Really, Olivia, there's nothing left to do. I'm just going to put these things in the dishwasher and then take Zeke for his walk."

"Okay," she said, dropping her dish towel on a chair. "I'll take Zeke out and you can go up and have first crack at the shower. Deal?"

Having heard his name pronounced in the same breath as the word "walk," Zeke trotted into the kitchen and looked eagerly from Jonas to Olivia.

"Okay. Just don't let that dog take you on a wild-goose chase, or I'll have to come out after you again. He has a bad habit of forgetting his name when it's time to turn around and come home."

"Don't worry, I can handle him," she said confidently, although she wasn't at all sure if she'd be back with the rambunctious canine before dawn. "See you in a few minutes," she said lightly as Zeke galloped ahead of her toward the back door.

Out on the dark beach, Olivia felt refreshed and revitalized. A cool breeze blew in off the pounding surf, swirling her hair in a wild disarray. She felt totally relieved that the Carmichaels' visit had just about come to an end. It hadn't been the least bit difficult playing Jonas's loving wife, but she was glad that they'd agreed that their act would be retired forever after tonight. The more she pretended to be married to Jonas, the more difficult it became to remind herself that he very well might not become a permanent part of her life.

Last night he had promised her a thousand times that everything would work out between them. But the man was no fortune teller, however sincere his intentions might be. She knew far too well that circumstances sometimes had a way of overpowering even the best intentions in a romantic relationship. There were far too many ifs still clouding their future for Olivia's peace of mind. Everything was still so tenuous and fragile between them. Although Jonas was certainly willing to demonstrate his desire for her at any opportunity, he still hadn't really made any admission of his feelings. All that will come in time, she thought, gazing out into the velvety blue-black expanse of sea and sky. She was just being impatient, her worst trait. Everything in this life was just a matter of timing.

Olivia's thought were interrupted by the sound of someone coming toward her. At first she thought it was Zeke romping around on the beach, when she looked up she could see it was a man. Her heart jumped hopefully at the thought that it might be Jonas, but soon she could tell that it was Brad.

"Sorry if I startled you. It sure is dark out here," he said, coming up beside her.

It was perfect weather for a stroll on the beach, but some instinctive inner warning system told her that Brad was not just out here for his nightly constitutional. "I was just thinking. I guess I didn't notice you coming."

He smiled at her. "A good night for thinking. Especially out here. Shall we walk a bit?" he asked, taking her elbow.

"Sure," Olivia said, having no real choice to do otherwise.

"I have to be honest with you. Marsha thinks I came down to walk off a little indigestion, but I knew you were down here and I followed you. I thought we should have a little time alone together. To talk.''

"To talk?" He was still holding on possessively to her elbow and Olivia could not quite figure out a graceful way of extricating herself from his grip. "What did you want to talk about?" Not more fishing stories, I hope, she silently added.

"You don't know?" He glanced at her questioningly and then looked away. "Well, I suppose I don't deserve for you to make it easy for me now—after the way I treated you at one time," he sighed.

Olivia suddenly understood that she was about to receive yet another heart-wrenching apology. She really wasn't used to so much groveling at her feet in one day. It made her nervous. Never before have so many apologized so often for so little, she thought to herself.

"Listen, Brad," she interrupted him, "if you're about to apologize for what happened when we were kids, just forget it, okay? As far as I'm concerned, it's really water under the bridge."

Brad glanced over at her and smiled. "Well, apologizing was only half of my little speech," he admitted. He stopped walking and glanced down at the sand. "Ever since running into you again in San Diego, I've thought a lot about what happened back then. About the mistake I made—"

"Brad you really don't have to say all this—"

"Just let me finish," he said, laying one hand gently on her arm. "The mistake I made in choosing Marsha over you, Olivia, is what I mean to say."

Olivia was stunned into silence for a moment. She realized in a flash why he had followed her out here and how sensitive a situation she was now tangled up in.

"You don't mean that, Brad," she replied firmly. "Marsha is a wonderful woman and anyone can see how happy you two are together," she insisted.

"Yes, Marsha has always been a fabulous wife and a perfect mother to our children," he said a bit remorsefully. "But she's different from you, Olivia—always was. Remember how I used to make fun of your friends from acting class and all those radical groups you belonged to?"

"Friends of the Whale was not exactly a revolutionary organization, Brad," she corrected him.

"See what I mean? That just goes to show what a pompous, uptight snob I was." He hung his head sadly and Olivia couldn't help feeling a tiny bit sorry for him. "Not that I'm any great liberal now," he added, taking off his glasses and wiping the lenses with the edge of his shirt. "But at least now I can see that I was just running scared from you, Olivia. You were just too much for a guy like me to handle . . . so strong minded and adventurous. I suppose I took the coward's way out and now I'm paying for it. I'd do anything to go back and change the past," he said fervently, his hands coming up to grip her shoulders. "It's still not too late you know—"

Olivia shook her head in dismay. "Brad, please. Get hold of yourself. Of course it's too late. We were never really right for each other. Time hasn't changed that...." She looked up at him to see if she was making an impression on him at all. It was difficult to tell but at least he had let go of her and she was able to take a step back.

"You think you've made some awful mistake and now you're pining away after me. It's not *me* you really miss, Brad. It's just that feeling you had—we all had—back then, of being so young and untried, with all our choices still ahead of us. Ready to conquer the business world, or become a big Broadway star. No matter what we do, we can never live that time ever again."

He looked out at the water. "I guess I know what you're trying to say," he admitted quietly. "Sure, I've felt a little nostalgic seeing you again. Who wouldn't? But honestly, it hasn't been just that. I feel something for you, I really do. I know you could feel it again, too, if you'd just let yourself."

He reached for her, but she pulled away from his grasp. "Brad, please. Don't act like this. Let's just go back to the house now, okay?" she said, turning around to look for Zeke.

"No...it's not okay, Olivia. I want you to remember how it was for us. I'm going to make you remember. I'm going to show you how good it still could be...."

Before Olivia could run, or even sound a word of protest, Brad had taken her in his arms and pressed his mouth forcefully over hers. Olivia's struggling and unwillingness to respond didn't dampen his ardor in the least, but it did cause them to lose their balance. Locked together they tumbled into the sand.

Olivia twisted and squirmed beneath him for a few moments, then finally wriggled free. Panting, she stood up shakily, trying to brush off the sand and rearrange her clothing. She was furious with Brad, but honestly didn't know how to handle the situation. She was sure that in the morning, his embarrassment over his behavior would be harsher reprisal than she could ever dish out at this moment.

Brad stood up slowly, feeling the first wave of humiliation for his foolishness, she had no doubt. She watched him warily and wondered what had become of Zeke the Wonder Dog while all this was going on. Wasn't that mongrel supposed to protect her from things like this? Then, a short distance down the shore she saw an outline of two figures, which she recognized as Zeke and Jonas. Jonas had probably come out after her just in time to witness the wrestling match with Brad. She was frankly grateful he had not decided to come to her aid. With his temper, there was no telling what might have happened.

Without so much as a wave of recognition, Jonas turned and started back toward the house with the dog. "Come on, Brad," Olivia called over her shoulder. "I think we should be getting back now."

Without saying a word, he trudged beside her. When the house came into view, Brad turned to her and began a stammering apology, but Olivia cut him short.

"Listen," she said, raising her hands in a signal of surrender, "I'm perfectly happy to forget all about this, if you are."

"You're too understanding," he said, sighing. "I really don't know what came over me...probably too much wine with dinner."

"Probably," Olivia agreed, grateful for any excuse at this point. "If we can't act a little foolish with old friends, who can we do it with?" she said with a shrug. She smiled and offered him her hand, but instead of shaking it, he raised it to his lips and gently dropped a kiss on her palm.

"Good night, old friend," he said gallantly. "I think I'll just sit out here for a spell if you don't mind. Remind me in the morning to tell Jonas what a lucky man he is."

"Good night, Brad," she said, retreating into the house. "See you tomorrow."

Olivia wearily climbed the stairs. The evening had certainly ended on a surprising note and she still had some explaining to Jonas ahead of her. She was sure that in a few minutes, however, they would both be laughing about the whole ridiculous episode.

She opened the bedroom to find Jonas propped up against the pillows, reading a book. He barely looked up at her when she came in and the expression on his face—or rather, the lack of one—made her stomach suddenly knot with alarm.

"Jonas," she said sitting on the edge of the bed, "put down that book and stop acting so silly. I know you saw me and Brad out there together and I want to explain what happened. It's really quite funny.''

"I saw what happened," he said, slamming the book shut and tossing it aside. "Extremely amusing," he agreed. "So—is it going to be a quickie divorce in Reno? Or is he just going to see you on the sly until he can square things away with dear old Marsha? A man with his assets has a lot at stake in this type of situation. Although I'm sure she'll walk away with a bundle. But you've finally shown her up after all this time, haven't you?"

"Shown her up? Reno? What in the world are you ranting about?" she asked, laughing at his outrageous accusations. "You have some imagination, Jonas, I must say that. But you don't have the slightest idea about what went on out there. You're not even warm.''

"Warm?" He bounded out of bed and pulled on his bathrobe. "You want to know about warm? That guy's been warm ever since he laid eyes on you in San Diego—he's been smoking. Tonight I thought he was just about to boil over." Jonas paced up and down in front of her in a manner that was almost hypnotizing. "And you didn't leave him alone for a second, not one second, Olivia. Laughing at all those boring fishing stories. Filling his glass, fixing his plate. I thought you were going to offer to cut his meat.''

"Of course I was attentive to him," she defended herself. "Somebody had to be. You were just about ignoring the man completely. I thought you were just nervous about the business deal, but I can see now that

I was sadly mistaken. You were jealous.'' Olivia could hardly believe that after all they had been through, Jonas had so little trust in her. She was hurt, and growing angrier by the second. But she knew that she had to try at least once more to make Jonas see reason. "I was only paying attention to Brad all night for your sake, can't you see that?''

"For my sake! That's a laugh, if I ever heard one,'' he said coldly. "Why, you engineered this fiasco from the start. But no hard feelings on my side, Olivia. We both got what we wanted out of this, didn't we? I've got the account with Multi-Foods and you've gotten your true love back. Tell you what, when the time comes, I'll even pretend to divorce you. Pretty fair-minded of me, don't you think?''

"Why you vile, despicable . . . How could you imagine that I could do such a thing? How could you think that I'd be capable of using you like that?'' she asked in a burst of outraged tears.

"Save those Academy Award-winning tears, sweetheart. You've tricked me for the last time,'' he assured her forlornly. "What a fool I was, worrying you would think that I was using you to get close to Carmichael. Why do you think I was so resistant to the idea of having them here? I was afraid you might have second thoughts and accuse me of taking advantage of our relationship, after all. Little did I know you had plans of your own.''

"I had no plans, Jonas. Except for helping you,'' she protested.

"Well, whether you figured on it or not, now you've gotten your long-lost love back. Congratulations, you've reeled in a prize catch and he certainly went for the bait, hook, line and sinker," he added snidely.

"Now that's the last straw. I won't stand here another moment and listen to this. If you honestly think I'm capable of such behavior, I don't want to have another thing to do with you, Jonas." Grabbing a pillow and a blanket off the bed, she proudly strode toward the door to the balcony. "I should have known this was a mistake from the very start."

"We both should have known," he called after her. "Go ahead, sleep out there if you want. Freeze your butt off. What do I care?" he grumbled to himself, sitting down hard on the bed with his arms crossed over his chest and his face set in a stubborn, brooding expression. "Do I care if you catch pneumonia?" he asked himself. "Not one little bit," she heard him answer as she made up a makeshift bed on a lounge chair.

Olivia went back inside and straight into the bathroom without even looking at him. Dressed in her nightgown and robe, she returned to her open-air bedroom. Wrapping herself in the blanket, she stretched out on the lounger. She felt lonely and full of despair. How had everything gone so sour so quickly? Surely Jonas would see how silly he was acting and come out to apologize to her. She hadn't slept outside like this since she was a girl and went camping in the backyard with her brother Todd. She hadn't liked it too much then, she recalled. She certainly didn't like it any more now. The light went off in Jonas's room with a very final-looking blink. Olivia hugged the blanket closer for warmth and looked up at the stars. Why in the world hadn't she waited for him to storm out here and leave her the bedroom? she wondered. Of all the stupid things she had done lately—and she had certainly done plenty—that had to have been the dumbest, she thought as she closed her eyes.

Seven

Olivia fought the urge to wave goodbye to Jonas. She sat in the back seat of the Carmichaels' rented car and clasped her hands around the edges of a script as Brad backed it down the long driveway. She also battled the urge to burst out crying. She didn't think that such a display would be a good way to begin the long drive to Los Angeles. Under any questioning at all from Marsha, she knew she would spill the whole story about her real relationship with Jonas. She didn't know why but she still felt some misguided loyalty to the pigheaded son of a gun.

She had awakened on the chaise longue feeling chilled and cramped. When she went into the bedroom, Jonas had just emerged from the shower. Once again, he refused to listen to her explanation about the night before, and she had finally given up. He dressed quickly and went downstairs to fix breakfast for Marsha and Brad. Olivia remained in the bedroom. Feeling hurt and rejected, she glumly considered her options.

A short time later, dressed in a crisp cotton outfit, she had joined the three of them at the breakfast table. It was a pleasure to watch the shocked expression on Jonas's face as she blithely announced that the Carmichaels were giving her a lift to Los Angeles. She had arranged everything with Marsha upstairs before getting dressed. Her bags were in the hallway ready to be loaded into the car. Her acting talents had really come in handy as she delivered the news with the sweetest of wifely smiles.

Jonas squirmed and coughed, trying to maintain the pose of her loving husband, while simultaneously trying to hide his surprise over her abrupt departure. Did the man honestly think she was going to remain under this roof one second more than was absolutely necessary? Did he think she was a glutton for abuse, for heaven's sake? Olivia had concocted a story about a sudden call from her agent and an unexpected opportunity for an audition. After all the misery Jonas had put her through in the past twelve hours, Olivia thought a little public discomfort was hardly punishment enough for his behavior.

Predictably, at one point Jonas had offered to drive her up to Los Angeles himself. But Olivia had casually brushed the offer aside while sending him a poisonous glance that left no doubt as to her real feelings about spending another minute in his company. She had to congratulate herself for timing the whole thing perfectly, and was barely able to finish a cup of coffee between the moment of her announcement and the time they were all saying their goodbyes. He had never known what hit him, she was sure.

A great showman to the last, however, he did manage to grab hold of her as she was striding out the front door for one last, soul-wrenching kiss. Waiting out by the car, Marsha and Brad naturally assumed that they were just saying farewell before a short business trip. Only Olivia and Jonas knew that they were saying their goodbyes for a lifetime.

As they broke apart, Jonas looked deeply into her eyes and for a second she believed that he was about to say he was sorry. Or at the very least, offer to talk things out. But he said nothing and she was simply too angry to make the first move this time. Pulling away from him, Olivia ran down the gravel walk and got into the car.

"Jonas looked lonely standing in the doorway when we pulled away," Marsha said once they were out on the freeway. "Too bad he couldn't come along."

Olivia looked up from the script she wasn't really reading. "Who wants him here?" she grumbled without thinking. She suddenly discovered Marsha looking at her quizzically and she rushed to cover her tracks. "I mean, I don't like to have Jonas around when I'm trying to concentrate on my work. It's boring for him and just too distracting for me."

"I can understand that," Marsha said, her look suggesting that she empathized far more than she was letting on. "I feel the same way about Brad when I go clothes shopping. There are times in a woman's life when having a man around just keeps her from concentrating the way she should."

It wasn't quite what she meant, but Olivia had to smile at Marsha's tidbit of feminine wisdom.

"Oh, dear, did I just hear the dreaded word 'shopping'?" Brad asked with mock alarm.

"You most certainly did, my pet," Marsha said cheerfully. "As a matter of fact, you can just drop me off on Rodeo Drive on the way to the hotel. I can find my own way back, I'm sure."

"Well at least you're not asking for the car. I suppose that's a good sign. How much can a person carry?" he speculated out loud.

"Nonsense, Brad darling." Marsha examined her manicure and adjusted the many gemstone rings that adorned her fingers. "Car... no car. What's the difference? Everyone knows all the better shops deliver."

"And deliver... and deliver... and deliver." Brad sighed. Yet Olivia could tell that he didn't mind Marsha's penchant for fine clothes. She was sure he wanted his wife to be well dressed and that all this bantering was just for show.

"Care to join me this afternoon, Olivia? It's been years since we made havoc of a dressing room together." Marsha turned around and gave her a conspiratorial wink.

Olivia laughed, recalling their shopping sprees in college. "Sounds very tempting, but I think I'll have to pass on this trip. I really have to study this script for my audition."

"Next time then," Marsha said amiably. "We'll be very good up here and try not to bother you. Won't we, dear?"

"Yes, dear," Brad agreed, catching Olivia's eye in the rearview mirror, his glance was one of friendly camaraderie. The awkwardness of the night before had been forgotten. In some strange way the crazy events of the past few days had served to renew her friendship with this couple in a very real way, Olivia realized. Although she still felt heartsick about Jonas, she did feel comforted by the new rapport that had evolved with her old friends.

It was pure coincidence that the three of them had made reservations in the same hotel. A coincidence, but decidedly a convenient one. After dropping Marsha off they checked in, and followed the bellman with their bags up to rooms that were directly across the hallway from each other. After tipping the bellman and closing the door, Olivia sank down in an armchair in an exhausted heap. It was almost noon, she noticed, late enough to call her agent in New York. It was Sunday morning, but this was an emergency. With any luck her agent could have the Tuesday audition moved up to tomorrow morning. Olivia wanted to get the darn thing over with and get out of California as fast as possible. She despised the entire state and everyone in it at that moment. Most particularly,

Jonas, especially since she realized that he knew where she was staying and hadn't even called her. How could she ever have thought for one minute that she could actually be happy in Los Angeles? And be happy with *him*, of all people, she thought furiously as she dialed her agent's home telephone number.

Marguerite Cummings didn't really understand why Olivia was in such a rush to get back to New York, but after twenty years of representing theatrical clients she certainly knew better than to try to reason with an overwrought actress. Trying to soothe Olivia as best as she could, she promised that she'd do everything possible to move the audition up.

With that problem settled, Olivia changed into her bathing suit and sundress and headed for the pool area to continue studying the script. The remainder of the day passed quickly as she alternated her character study with laps in the oval-shaped pool. Just to pamper herself, she had her hair trimmed and blow-dried in the hotel's ritzy salon. It cost more money than she could really afford and didn't help lift her spirits much, but she knew she had to look her best for the cameras tomorrow. Sleeping on a chaise longue last night hadn't done much for her appearance, that was for sure.

More than once, she reached for the phone to dial Jonas's number, but stopped herself at the last minute. She wasn't going to be the first one to apologize. If he trusted her so little and couldn't admit what a fool he had been, then she didn't need him. And the sentiment went double for that ridiculous dog.

With such thoughts swirling around in her head, Olivia ordered herself a salad from room service and then went straight to bed. As soon as she shut off the light, however, she began to cry and just couldn't stop. Cursing Jonas doubly for the problems he caused her, she jumped out of bed and again called room service, asking them to send up a cold sliced cucumber and some ice. She couldn't have her eyes looking all puffy and swollen in the morning. With her head propped up on three pillows and a pile of cucumber slices over each eye, she once again tried to get some sleep. She once more felt the urge to cry when she shut out the light, but picturing what she looked like, she honestly felt too ridiculous for any more tears.

The next morning, a car arrived from the television studios to take Olivia to the audition. She was greeted warmly by the producer and then introduced to other executives—the director and writers—and then, to the show's other cast members. The producer and director both seemed very sure that she was the actress they had been looking for, and their confidence in her abilities gave Olivia a much-needed boost. She had never pursued a role in a comedy before and had been talked into this audition by Marguerite. She felt some trepidation, knowing she'd feel terrible if she delivered her lines and nobody laughed. But when she stepped out under the lights, she was once again able to forget all her worries and concentrate on delivering a good performance. As she had once told Jonas, acting was often a great relief because it allowed a person to forget his own troubles by jumping into someone else's skin for a while. It was certainly one of those days for Olivia, who took on her comedic role with relish.

If the chuckles from the stage crew were any indication of her ability to deliver comic lines with punch, it seemed that Olivia's worries had been needless. When the taping concluded, the entire crew and the studio executives looking on gave the cast a loud round of applause. Olivia looked around as if she had just woken up from a dream. The audition had concluded, she realized, and the results were more than hopeful.

After speaking briefly with the show's producer, Olivia floated off the set on a cloud of euphoria. She felt much too elated to return to the hotel and asked the studio driver to drop her off at Chasen's—a fancy Beverly Hills eatery where she treated herself to lunch and looked for movie stars.

She soon ran out of ways to divert herself, however. Her buoyant mood was overcome little by little by a cloud of sadness. Walking back toward the hotel, she realized that the only thing that would make her really happy was a message from Jonas waiting for her when she got back. A message was handed over by the desk clerk upon her arrival, but when Olivia eagerly opened the folded slip of paper, she felt her heart sink. It was from Marguerite, not Jonas as she had hoped, asking her to phone right away.

"Hello, Olivia? Great news!" Marguerite shouted into the line. "The producer of the sitcom called immediately after your audition. They're ready to make a deal, honey, and I think you're going to be very pleased when you hear the kind of money they're offering just for openers."

"I'm so surprised, I don't know what to say." Olivia sat down on the bed, feeling quite shocked. She knew she'd done a good job that morning, but she'd hardly expected a response from the studio so soon. "This is all rather quick, isn't it? Are you sure it's a firm offer?"

"After all these years in the business, believe me honey, I know a firm offer when I hear one. That show goes into production any minute. We really have them over a barrel. We might even have to get you killed off sooner than expected in *All Our Tomorrows*." Marguerite pondered out loud. "But don't you worry, dear. I'll work it all out. That's what I'm here for. Farewell Soapville... Hello prime time."

As she had often observed before, Olivia believed that her agent's real talents had been wasted on the business end of acting. Marguerite always had a way of making the most of her lines.

"Well, honey? Are you still there? You're not turning mellow on me already, are you?" Marguerite rattled on at her breakneck rate. "If the deal goes through—and it will," she assured her, "then of course they'll want to meet with you just about every day next week."

"So I'll have to stay put for a while I guess," Olivia said glumly.

"You're darn right you will. It looks like you're going to be there for a while, so you had better get used to it, Olivia. By the way, I've had a bottle of champagne sent up to your room so you could celebrate. Have fun tonight and call me in the morning."

No sooner had Olivia said goodbye when a sharp knock sounded on the door. It was room service with her champagne. Olivia allowed the waiter to open the bottle for her and then gave him too big a tip. She poured herself a glass of the effervescent wine as if it was medicine she really didn't want to take but had to. It was hard to celebrate something this momentous alone. She knew that the Carmichaels were right across the hall, but she wasn't really in the mood for their company. It was only Jonas's voice she wanted to hear right now, and she knew that she couldn't enjoy her success, or have a minute's peace of mind, until their misunderstanding was settled.

Sitting on the bed with her feet up, she poured herself a second glass of champagne, then pulled the phone into her lap and started dialing. The phone rang and rang, but there was no answer. She hung up and tried again. Thinking she might have misdialed, she called information to check the number. Working her way though a considerable number of glasses of champagne, Olivia dialed and redialed until her fingertip was numb.

"Some celebration," she mumbled to herself, leaning back against the pillows. The sun had nearly set and she didn't bother to put on the light. "Some swinging West Coast party," she said with a sigh.

Without realizing it, she slipped off into a deep, champagne-induced sleep.

Olivia opened her eyes in the pitch-dark hotel room. There was a pounding on the door that matched the one inside her head. Her mouth felt dry and cottony and her legs like a mismatched set as she stumbled toward the door.

"I'm coming. I'm coming," she complained to her unseen visitor. She had sudden hope that it was Jonas, but when she swung open the door all she found on the other side was her old friend Brad.

"Olivia, thank goodness you're all right. Marsha and I got worried. We've been trying to call you for hours but the line was busy."

"I was just taking a little nap," she explained, running a hand over her sleep-rumpled outfit. "Come on in," she told him. She walked over to the bed and, following the phone line from the wall, managed to locate the rest of the equipment under the tangle of sheets and pillows. "Here it is," she said, placing the phone back on the night table. "I always disconnect the phone for a nap," she said lightly.

"Not that I'm trying to be nosy...but do you always order yourself a bottle of Dom Perignon before napping as well?" he asked with friendly concern.

"My usual drink is chamomile tea," she said dryly. She suddenly realized that he thought she either had a drinking problem, or had been entertaining a gentleman caller. "I just got a part in a television series and I was celebrating," she explained, wondering why she sounded so awfully glum over such news.

"That's fabulous," Brad congratulated her. "I'll bet Jonas is thrilled."

"I haven't told him yet," she said tersely.

"Olivia, forgive me for prying but is anything wrong between you and Jonas?" Brad asked sympathetically. "He certainly didn't seem himself as we were leaving the house yesterday."

Olivia looked up at him. She didn't have the energy for any more fabrications, and she was certainly badly in need of a sympathetic ear. "Tell the truth, Brad, Jonas saw you and me together on the beach and he didn't *quite* understand what happened." She nervously looked up at him.

"Oh, dear. You mean my foolish antics have been the cause of this? I'm so sorry, Olivia. I'll call him at once and explain everything," he said, resolutely heading for the phone.

"I don't know if that's such a good idea, Brad. Maybe you should wait a few days until he's cooled down. Jonas can have a frightful temper. He's really not to be reasoned with. If he even suspected that we were alone together in the room like this, I don't know what he'd do."

Brad looked at her thoughtfully. "Well, whatever you say, Olivia. I suppose you know him best. He's your husband," he added, to which Olivia made no comment.

"Won't you let us take you out for dinner? We can celebrate... your new job and a start to our new friendship."

Olivia sat down wearily on the bed. "I don't know, Brad. I don't feel all that great, to tell the truth."

"Oh, come on now," Brad cajoled her. "We want to thank you, Olivia, Marsha and I. Meeting up with you has really helped us. In ways you probably can't imagine. You were so right that night on the beach when I made an idiot out of myself. I do love Marsha, and now we feel closer than ever. There were some ghosts in our marriage, you might say," he admitted. "But now we've been able to put them all to rest. Thanks to you, Olivia."

"Okay," she relented, seeing how sincere he seemed. "I guess I'll go get ready."

"Great." Taking her by the arm, he ushered her toward the bathroom. "Better hurry. Marsha's been debating all day of which of her new frocks she's going to wear. I have a feeling she'll be over any minute to try them all on for you."

Olivia felt herself pushed gently across the threshold and the bathroom door firmly closed behind her. She walked up to the mirror and then stuck out her tongue at herself. "I look like a car wreck," she muttered to herself. "Without the car." Shaking her head, she sighed and began to undress. At least dinner with the Carmichaels would take her mind off Jonas for a while, she thought as she turned on the shower.

When Olivia emerged from the shower, she could hear someone banging on the door to her hotel room. She quickly grabbed the robe that was hanging on the door and opened the door a crack to peek out.

"Brad?" she called into the apparently empty room. "Want to get the door?"

The room was not all that large and Brad was clearly not in sight, she discovered upon opening the bathroom door wider once she had her robe on. The pounding on the front door had stopped momentarily, but as she ran to open it, the noise continued anew. This time accompanied by a familiar, belligerent voice.

"All right, all right," she said as she worked on the lock. "What in the world are you making such a racket out here for?" she asked as she flung open the door. Olivia couldn't believe her eyes. It was Jonas! She was delighted to see him, but hardly had a chance to say hello, or to say anything, for that matter. As soon as the door was open, he swept past her and started looking around the room as if he was searching for an escaped criminal. All he needed to make the impression complete, was a leashed bloodhound.

"All right ... where is he? Where are you hiding him?"

"Jonas, for heaven's sake, aren't you going to even say hello?" she asked him, noticing for the first time that he was carrying the most tremendous bouquet of flowers she had ever seen. "Where's *who*?" she asked in total confusion.

"Who do you think?" he asked her, coming up to stand directly in front of her. "I heard both of you scrambling around while I was cooling my heels on the other side of that door. Look at this place," he said, waving his battle-torn bouquet at the disarrayed bed and bottle of champagne. "Don't even try to deny that he's been here this time, Olivia. It would be absolutely pointless."

Olivia grabbed at her head in utter frustration. How did these things keep happening to her? "Yes, Brad has been here," she practically moaned. "But this is not what you think," she said apathetically, knowing that her words were going in one ear and out the other. "Why don't you just sit down a minute and . . ."

"I will do no such thing," he said, stepping clear of the chair she offered and circling the room again as if he could actually sniff the culprit out.

"Jonas, please pay attention to what I'm saying," she said firmly. "Read my lips. Brad Carmichael is not—I repeat *not* in this room."

Jonas, who had been lifting back a curtain, turned and looked at her. For an instant, she truly believed he was about to calm down and at least pretend to hear her out. Then, as she and Jonas stared at each other across the silent hotel room, somebody quite clearly sneezed. It wasn't either of them. Jonas's expression turned from borderline mollification to that of a wounded bull on the loose. In an instant he had sprinted across the room to the closet, where a second sneeze sounded. He flung open the door and Brad stumbled out into the room, his face partly obscured by a handkerchief.

"Aha!" Jonas said with the glee of a hunter who has cornered his prey.

"Ah-choo," Brad replied, sneezing again into his hankie, his watery eyes wide with alarm.

"Oy-veh," Olivia said, plunking herself down in an armchair as though she had totally given up on trying to make any sense of the situation.

"Oh, it's just his silly allergies acting up again. He knows he should take his medication, but does he?" Before anyone could say another word, Marsha stepped out of the closet, wearing no more than a thin, lace-trimmed, satin dressing gown. "Here I am pushed in the closet for what I think is going to be a little fun and games, and the man just sneezes all over me," she complained to nobody in particular. "Jonas! It's so wonderful that you could join us in our little celebration tonight!" she rattled on cheerfully. "What luck that we didn't start without you, isn't it, Olivia?" she asked her friend.

Without answering Marsha, Olivia turned to Jonas with a wide smile on her face. Dumbstruck by this latest turn of events, Jonas looked at the three of them, unable to say a word. Olivia could only begin to imagine the lurid thoughts that must have been spinning around his brain. It served him right, she thought with spiteful satisfaction. "Well, Sherlock?" she finally asked him. "Just what do you make of this now?"

Suddenly a waiter appeared at the open doorway carrying a silver tray and a covered dish. "Room service?" he asked hesitantly.

"Come on in," Olivia replied, waving him forward. "The more the merrier, that's what I always say," she said, glancing at Jonas. Without thinking, she quickly signed the check and the waiter departed, leaving the tray on a small table near the bed. When she lifted up the cover, all she found was a jar of chocolate syrup in a silver serving bowl. "What in the world . . . Who ordered this?"

"I did, you idiot," Jonas said crossly. Tossing down his bouquet of flowers in disgust, he crossed his arms sullenly over his chest and sat down on the little stool in front of the dressing table.

"Marsha, dear, I think we had better leave our friends alone for some married-people talk." With an understanding smile Brad smoothly ushered his partially clad wife toward the door.

"Oh...of course," Marsha said as politely as if she was departing from a formal tea. "Just let me get my things," she added, dashing back into the room to scoop up an armful of dinner outfits that were draped over a chair, the tags still hanging from the sleeves. "I think I may wear the blue silk after all," she said quite solemnly.

"Let's discuss it in our room, shall we?" With an apologetic smile, Brad ushered his wife through the door and they made a swift exit.

Olivia and Jonas were now completely alone and the silence was almost deafening.

"I guess you're expecting some kind of explanation," she began with a weary sigh. "You didn't believe me the other night . . . you wouldn't even listen. Do you think I should even bother trying to explain this one?" she asked him point-blank.

"Olivia...I don't know what went on here tonight, but frankly I don't think I really care right now."

"You don't?" she echoed, feeling mildly shocked.

He shook his head. "You heard me right. The other night I acted like a complete idiot. I've been miserable since you left and I have only one excuse for making a fool of myself," he said, coming toward her. "I just love you so much. That's all I really came here tonight to say."

Olivia moved toward him and wrapped her arms around his waist. "I love you, too, Jonas," she said, leaning her head back for his kiss. "I can explain all this, believe me," she assured him.

"Great. You can tell me all about it...later," he instructed, leaning over to sweep her up in his arms. In two great strides he had reached the bed, where he unceremoniously dumped her on the rumpled pile of blankets and bedraggled flowers. "All I want you to tell me right now is that you love me again," he said, pulling loose his tie, "and the only thing I'm going to tell you is why I had that chocolate sauce sent up," he added with a wicked but loving gleam in his eye.

A few hours later, they sat propped up against the pillows wrapped in each other's arms.

"Well, I guess dear old Marsha and Brad just had to paint the town without us tonight," Jonas said with a contented grin. "We'll have to thank them for leaving us alone to settle our differences next time we get together."

"Yes, we will, won't we?" she said, snuggling closer and resting her cheek on his chest. Now that all their explaining and apologizing was out of the way, it felt good to just relax and look forward to the future that looked brighter than ever.

"I think it's high time we ended all this fooling around and stopped pretending to be married in front of them, Olivia."

"You do?" She lifted her head to look at him. "I don't know, Jonas. I really don't care anymore whether they think I got married or not. But what if Brad gets angry when he finds out? Couldn't it ruin your deal? Maybe we should just keep up the act when they're around."

"No, that's final," Jonas contradicted her quite firmly. "I refuse to pretend to be your husband ever again, Olivia. I guess you'll just have to make an honest man of me...."

"Does that mean I passed the audition?" she teased, flinging her arms around his neck.

"It certainly does...and the contract's for life. Think you're interested?" he asked quite seriously.

"Sounds like an attractive deal to me." She smiled and kissed the tip of his nose. "My agent will call you later in the week to talk it over in more detail," she said nonchalantly.

"Good. We've got better things to do right now than talk." He leaned over and clicked off the light.

Silhouette Desire

**Available
January 1987**

NEVADA
SILVER

The third book in the exciting
Desire Trilogy by Joan Hohl.

The Sharp brothers are back, along with
sister Kit... and Logan McKittrick.

Kit's loved Logan all her life and, with a little
help from the silver glow of a Nevada night,
she must convince the stubborn rancher that
she's a woman who needs a man's love—not
the protection of another brother.

Don't miss *Nevada Silver*—Kit and
Logan's story and the conclusion
of Joan Hohl's acclaimed
Desire Trilogy.